# RETURN TO VIKKI

# RETURN TO VIKKI

JOHN TOMERLIN

CUTTING EDGE

ISBN-13: 978-1-962896-14-6

Published by
Cutting Edge Books
PO Box 8212
Calabasas, CA 91372
www.cuttingedgebooks.com

# CHAPTER ONE

LATER HE WOULD THINK of this day and make of each swift second—each swift, normal, humdrum second—a separate memory. He would call back all the fresh, clean smells, the sights and quiet sensations, and feed on them. For these were the moments that would pass before doomsday.

Now they did not exist; they had no significance. There should have been a soft drum-roll in the distance, but there wasn't—only the neighborhood street.

He stepped down from the Mission Avenue bus and watched the old machine depart in a wash of blue-gray smoke. Tossing his coat over his shoulder and shifting his leather briefcase, he started the short, delicious walk toward home. It was one of those warm summer afternoons in Blaine, Ohio when everything seemed a little brighter than life, and by the time he'd reached his street he had begun to whistle softly to himself. It was not until he turned the corner and began walking the last half block that he saw the automobile parked in front of his home. He stopped whistling abruptly.

The flat-carved angles of Frank's face formed a frown, and he slowed his pace. The car was not familiar, yet for some reason the sight of it disturbed him. It was a large, dark-colored sedan he could not recall seeing before. As he drew near, he noticed that the car bore New York license plates, and his feeling of apprehension grew deeper. He gave a mental shrug at his nervousness as he turned in at the walk—friend of Nancy's, probably, or someone visiting the Jaspersons across the street.

The Shelby home was medium-sized, brown, with a flagstone base, surrounded by a pleasant lawn dotted with shrubs. The place was a little too large for just Nancy and himself, but when they'd bought it nearly four years ago they had hoped there would be children. Nancy was waiting for him at the door. He went up the steps.

"Is this the residence of the fabulously beautiful Mrs. Frank Shelby?" he said, circling her waist with one arm. "You'll be interested to know that that dolt of a husband of yours lost you on an election bet … I'm here to collect." She laughed and let him kiss her standing in the doorway. Then she drew away, and he saw her gray eyes were serious. "What's the matter, don't want to welsh on a bet, do you?"

"I was afraid you were going to be late," she said, her delicately molded face solemn, the way it looked when she was worried. "There's a man here to see you."

"Mmm—felt like walking today," he explained, coming in and closing the door. "Got off the bus one stop early. Who's here?"

"He says he's a friend of yours, a Mr. Benson."

Frank paused in the hallway, something freezing inside him. *Arnold Benson.*

So it's come at last, he thought dully. And this is the way it happened … no mysterious letter, no phone call, no whisper from the shadows. Just an "old friend," stopping in to say hello and pass the time of day.

After five long years.

He heard Nancy go into the closet behind him and rested his weight momentarily against the small hat-table. He pressed the bridge of his nose with his fingers. Five years seemed so short now—an instant, a split-second; yet in that time he'd found everything he had used to hunger for in the frightened, twisted part of his life that had gone before. His wife, a job, a town to live in—everything.

For a long time, in the beginning, after he had come to Blaine, he had wondered *what if?* He had started at every unexpected sound, answering each ring of the phone with a tortured dread. But after a while the fear had become less; he'd forgotten to wonder and be afraid. The normal, everyday things left no time for the past. Now the past was back, claiming its due. He thought of this and all the other forgotten fragments—plans for escape, schemes for what to do. Then he forced the useless memories from his mind. It was too late. The time for thinking was past, the time to act had arrived. Pulling his body erect, he walked down the hall and into the front room.

"Frank! My God, boy, how are you!" The man sitting on the couch got up and came forward, a massive figure, taller by a head than his host and fifty pounds heavier. His bulk seemed out of proportion in the neat, attractively furnished living room, dwarfing normal-sized tables and chairs. *Big Arnie.*

Shelby hesitated a moment, then, conscious of his wife's eyes on him, forced out his hand. "Hello ... Benson," he said.

The big man gripped him in a thick paw. "It's been a long time, boy, a real long time. But you're looking good, yessir! Mighty good."

"Thanks."

"By golly, the times we've thought about you and talked about you, and here you are, never letting us hear a word about how you're getting along." Benson sat down again on the couch, his full grin baring two rows of stubby, bad teeth. Frank stood a moment, then turned a chair around to face his guest. "Make yourself at home," he said.

Nancy paused long enough to see them settled, then said, "I'll make coffee," and went out to the kitchen.

Benson leaned back, his eyes following the girl. "Quite a little lady you got there," he said, nodding his huge head. It was pendulous, shaped like a partly deflated football, folding at the bottom into a series of swollen chins. Small, colorless eyes looked out from under ridged brows, and two strands of hair lay pasted

3

against the sides of his head, trailing back from the narrow, balding brow. He regarded Frank with faint mockery. "Guess you weren't expecting to see me, eh, Connor?" he said softly.

"Cut that!" Shelby snapped. "You know my name."

The big man nodded, undisturbed. "That's right," he said. "I do."

"How did you find me?"

"Not easy," Benson said, taking a cigar from his coat pocket and beginning to strip off the wrapper. He wet the end of it carefully, rolling the tip between his extended lips. "It took a long time, and we weren't even sure it was you when we got the tip. We've got lots of bum leads in the time we was hunting."

"You must have wanted to find me pretty bad."

The other nodded. "Spent a lot of dough, but it finally paid off. Guy out here working with the truck organizers spotted your picture in the paper—big write-up, something to do with a partnership?"

Shelby nodded. It had happened a while back, Jim Avery's little surprise for him, announcing his appointment as junior member of the firm; there'd been a party, a small reception with some publicity in the local papers. He'd been flattered. He swore inwardly, now, remembering how hard he'd tried to avoid just such a slip over the years. "I still don't get it, Benson," he said. "If you wanted me that bad, there must be a reason."

Nancy came back into the room with the coffee and a dish of cookies.

"Say, these are plenty good, Mrs. Shelby," Benson said, biting off half of a large cookie. "Made 'em yourself, I'll bet."

Nancy smiled. "Yes—thank you."

"Honey, we were talking some business—"

"Oh, that's all right," Benson interrupted. "I don't mind speaking with the ladies around. Nothing secret," he said, turning to address Nancy directly, "about the fact I'm trying to steal your husband from his job."

Frank glanced at the big man threateningly. "Mr. Benson is with a construction firm—in New York," he said. "He, uh, had a deal in mind for me."

Benson looked at him with pleasure. "That's right," he agreed. "Old Frank here is just the man we need. I mean he's got a lot on the ball. As a matter of fact, I know a couple of pretty big outfits back East that would just love to get their hands on him," he said, grinning.

The first raw edge of a threat.

"Yes," Nancy said, "we've always thought he could do well in a larger community." Her voice was careful, polite, feeling her way.

"*That's* it—big city, big opportunities for a man with talent! I know all about Frank. We used to work together—for the same man."

Nancy glanced at her husband.

"I'm afraid I never mentioned anything about that to Nan," he said. "We don't talk much about what I did before I came to Blaine."

"Yeah? Well, I'm kind of hurt you never told her about me," Benson said, chuckling, pulling at his cigar. "But anyway, we got a big proposition cooking and Frank's about the only guy I know can swing it for us." He shook his head wonderingly. "I never seen anybody could organize things the way your husband can, Mrs. Shelby. He's a regular genius some ways."

Okay, Benson, Frank thought, you can drop it, now. You've made it real clear. I get it. Now lay off before Nan figures out what kind of a slimy skunk you are and starts wondering why I don't throw you out into the gutter where you belong.

Frank glanced sharply across the room, and after a moment his wife stood up. "Darling, I'm awfully sorry," she said. "I promised Mrs. Jasperson I'd come over for a few minutes and watch the children while she picks up her husband." She turned to Benson. "Will you excuse me just a little while?"

The heavy man rose. "Why, certainly, Mrs. Shelby, you go right ahead. I imagine this shop talk is pretty dull for you anyway."

After Nancy had gone, Benson remained standing. He took a heavy, onyx-initialed lighter from his coat and applied it to the cold end of his cigar. Slowly, he moved around the Shelbys' front room. "Nice place you got here, Connor." He paused to admire the Degas reproduction above the mantel.

"I told you my name is—"

"Sure, sure. Sorry," he said. "Don't mind if I smoke?"

"Let's get down to it," Frank said thinly.

Benson came back to the couch and lowered himself to the brown-and-charcoal-striped cushions. "I've got to hand it to you, boy, you've done real good for yourself. Nice house, pretty wife—though she ain't no Vikki, of course." He snapped his blunt fingers. "Hey, that's right, Vikki said to say hello to you. You know," he said thoughtfully, "that was kind of a dirty trick you played on her. Walking out the way you did."

Shelby was tense, leaning forward now, his body shaking with anger. "Arnie—"

"Good job you got, too, from what the paper said." His eyes traveled around the room, taking in the tan and cocoa walls, the thick, soft beige carpet, the carefully picked chairs and drapes in accenting shades of blue and tangerine. "Yeah, things must be real fine."

Frank controlled himself carefully. "That's right," he said, "they are real fine. And they're going to *stay* real fine." He handed an ashtray over to Benson, who was looking around for a place to drop the tip of his cigar. "You want me to do a job for you, right? Just like old times?" He laughed. "Well, forget it. Forget all about it, Benson, like the idea never even entered your mind. I like it here, and this is where I'm staying, so unless you've got something else pretty important on your mind I'd suggest you get the hell out of here."

The big man brushed a pearl-colored ash into the dish Shelby had given him. "Take it easy, boy," he said gently. "Sure, it's going to stay good for you. We don't want to mess anything up—that's one of the things Mr. Hanford said I should be sure to tell you."

"*Hanford!*" The name struck like a doubled fist. "What's he got to do with this?"

Big Arnie shrugged. "Hell, he's still running things, boy."

Shelby stood up, now, his face twisting. Surprised, Benson pulled to his feet.

"That's where you're wrong," Frank said harshly. He took a half step forward and stopped at a noise from the hall. Nancy was standing in the archway, staring at them.

"Is—is everything all right?" She came slowly into the room. "Mr. Jasperson got a ride from the office, so I didn't have to stay."

Frank found his voice first. He laughed uneasily. "Sure, honey. Everything's fine. Let's have a little more coffee, can we? My cup's empty."

She hesitated, then went out to get the coffee pot.

The heavy man smoothed the palms of his hands against his coat lapels. "Better take things easy Mr., uh, Shelby," he said, nodding toward the other room. Frank's jaw muscles knotted but he didn't answer. Benson went on: "Just don't get the idea we ain't serious. We need help on a deal, boy, and we've got one all lined up. For a guy like you it's a candy cane, and all we want is just this one."

Frank made a short noise. "Don't strain yourself, Arnie. Who're you talking to, your kid sister?"

Benson rolled the cigar in his mouth. It had gone out, but he didn't seem to notice. "You don't want to be that way, boy," he said. "You're not going to leave me any choice. I got it plain— either you talk business with Mr. Hanford or we close the book on you—get what I mean?"

In the silence between them, Nancy re-entered with the coffee.

"I'm sorry, Mrs. Shelby," Benson said, turning, "but I'm going to have to pass up seconds this time. When you gotta go—" He looked at Frank. "You consider our little proposition. I think you'd be smart to at least come out and talk things over with Mr. Hanford before you make up your mind for sure." He moved toward the door.

Nancy brought the big man's coat from the hall closet. "I'm sorry you can't stay for dinner, Mr. Benson," she said in a voice that did not sound sorry.

"So am I, mam, if those cookies were a fair sample of what I'm going to miss. But there's some things I got to clear up in town before I leave, and it's getting late." He faced Frank again. "Tell you what, I'll give you a call about ten o'clock tonight. You let me know what you decide." He narrowed his eyes slightly. "We got to know pretty quick, because, like I say, there's these other outfits that are interested in Frank and the word may get out where to find him. They'd sure try to beat us to him. They haven't forgot a couple little jobs he worked on last time he was back East."

For a minute Shelby didn't trust himself to speak, then he said, "I'll think about it, Benson … nice to see you again."

"Sure was, Frankie. And you, too, Mrs. Shelby. A pleasure. So long, now." His big back cut off the light from the door a brief second, then he was down the steps heading for his car. The engine of the dark-colored sedan sounded, and in a moment it was gone from the quiet street.

Frank closed the door and let his breath escape through clenched teeth. Only then did he realize he'd been holding it for some time. Nancy had gone back to the front room. She was gathering up the soiled dishes, emptying Benson's cigar ashes into the dregs of one of the cups, moving them toward the kitchen. He watched her working, admiring the ease with which she carried herself. She turned, hands filled with dishes, and looked at him. Suddenly uncomfortable, he avoided her gaze and went across the room to pull the blinds and switch on a light. It was growing dark.

Nancy said nothing until they were finishing dinner that night. "A little different from what I expected your friends to be like." Her tone told him nothing.

"We were never very close," he said.

"Is everything all right, Frank?"

"What? Oh, sure, Nan, fine." Her eyes held his until he looked away again. "It was just business, Nan, believe me. It's nothing for you to worry about."

"But not *my* business, you mean?" He looked down without answering. She didn't say anything else either, but he knew she wasn't satisfied—he hadn't deceived her. He would have to do better, invent something that would get by until he had more time to think.

"Look, Nan, I'm sorry. Of course it's your business. The fact is, Benson had a proposition for me, a—a construction deal back East, lot of money. I don't know if I want it." He found the lie coming hard. "We've had it pretty good here, you know."

"Is it something you don't want to do, Frank?"

"Well, I guess you could say that." He thought of the life he'd built, the job he liked, and the people who liked him. He remembered Jim Avery, who had given him a chance to prove himself when he'd just come into town—his first real chance—and how he'd seized it with the eagerness of a desperate man.

Avery had taken the young stranger into his architectural office with no more references than the fact that Frank remembered from high school days what a drafting board was for. That had been the start, the beginning of five good years. ...

"Darling, don't worry about this. I'll work it out. I think I'll go to my room for a while." He'd had an idea—a wild hope, perhaps, but one which might get them out of it yet. She nodded, the worried lines on her face relaxing a little, giving him a half smile of encouragement.

"All right, Frank," she said. "Whatever you want is what I'll want, too."

He sat down in his chair and picked up the phone eagerly, excitement beginning in him. Money first—yes, money, and then just a little time. He dialed Jim Avery's home. The telephone rang steadily, monotonously. At last he cursed and slammed the receiver down. At a dinner party or a card game or some damn thing; why the hell couldn't a man like that stay home once in a while? He was getting old, he'd have a heart attack one of these days and—

There was Elliot Collier, Nancy's father. He had money. A deal like this, a "quiet vacation" for his daughter and son-in-law, would appeal to him—but no. Collier mustn't be dragged into this.

He sat, staring at the telephone on the table before him, knowing it was only a matter of minutes now. Seconds, maybe. At last as he had known it would, the telephone jangled. Slowly, he picked it up and held it to his ear.

"That you, Frank?"

He hesitated.

"You there, Frank?"

"Yes, I'm listening."

"Good. Make up your mind what you want to do?"

He thought, I can't afford to make a mistake. I've got to figure this right, just exactly right. Benson hasn't got the say-so—if I tell him no, he'll just call the cops. But if it's yes, then I've got to face Hanford. I need time. I've got to figure everything out. I've got to think.

"How about it?" the voice insisted. He closed his eyes. Only a little time, he thought. God help me. Then he moved the receiver closer to his mouth. "All right," he said softly. "When do you think Mr. Hanford would be able to see me?"

# CHAPTER TWO

H E WAS BEING SWEPT down the river, his tiny boat rocking and pitching in the black, roiling water. Clutching the gunwales, he moved from side to side to keep from going over, but ahead he could already hear the roar of the rapids and see the raging white froth pierced by looming monster-shapes of rocks, hard and cold, waiting to dash him to death. He could not escape, the current was too strong.

Frank Shelby jerked upright in the seat, his hands griping the cushions of the car. It was raining outside, and the sound of tires on pavement was a wet hiss, like swiftly moving water. It was dark now, the headlights fighting their way through sheets of gray, reflecting water, picking out the dim ribbon of road. Frank glanced at the driver, saw Benson's head turn slowly toward him on the almost invisible fat neck. The big man's eyes, glowing with the yellow light of the dashboard, surveyed him with amusement.

"Sleep?"

"Guess so," he said, looking at his watch. The luminous hands pointed to eleven o'clock.

"We're about there now," Benson said, nodding ahead. A few minutes later, a large neon sign appeared to the right of the road in front of them. Frank watched it grow clearer through the rain until he could make out the word XANADU in block Arabian-looking letters, and, then, CLUB above it in smaller lights. He stirred himself, feeling stiff and chilled.

"Is that the place?"

"That's it," Benson said.

"Looks fancy."

The big building took shape in the night. Drowning flood-lights cut upwards through the moisture-filled air, outlining the club's massive form against the blackness. The front of the build-ing was very modern, mostly glass and stone, with a diagonal line of bas-relief figures climbing one cement-blocked wall.

The car cut down from the crown of the road, slowing, to roll across a wide parking lot and come to a stop underneath the shelter of a broad portico. A man in a yellow rain-slicker and a glistening cap stepped to Benson's door and opened it for him.

Frank got out on his side, shivering in the sudden blast of air that whipped through the open ends of the portico but glad of the protection of the roof overhead. He waited for Benson to join him. Then they walked up the steps and in through the automati-cally operated glass doors.

The interior of the club was lavish, vast and dimly lit, filled with the sound of faint music and crowded with well-dressed people. Walls of deeply polished wood reflected the moving fig-ures and picked up the dark red and blue casts of the carpet. A cavernous ceiling arched overhead. As they entered, a swarthy-skinned man in white robes came forward. He bowed deeply, offering to take their coats.

"You can tell them we're here," Benson said. The robed man nodded and went away. Arnie motioned for Frank to follow and led the way across the lobby and in through a heavily curtained arch.

Frank suddenly felt as though he had been transported to another world. He blinked his eyes, trying to remember that only a few hours before he had been in the quiet town of Blaine, Ohio. Now he seemed to have traveled several thousand miles in the passing of an instant. To all appearances, they were in the midst of a desert oasis, surrounded by sand and trees.

"Hanford hangs out here?" Frank asked.

Benson chuckled. "You might say that—he owns the place." He motioned with one hand. "We can wait at this table."

They sat down on low, luxurious beds of cushions, cradled comfortably a few inches off the floor. The polished mahogany tables were sculptured to fit close to the body. Here, in the main club-room, the cavernlike effect had been carried to fulfillment. The floor sloped gently downward to a wide central area, strewn with what looked like large boulders, beyond which was a small pool of water edged with white sand. The ceiling vaulted into darkness, but across it were scattered thousands of tiny points of light—like stars. Suddenly he realized that that's what they were supposed to be—the whole effect was of a tremendous grotto, cupped beneath limitless sky.

Frank looked around and saw that a girl was standing beside their table.

"May I have your order, please?" she said in a low, musical voice. She was dressed like an East Indian dancing girl in bright silk pantaloons and filmy jacket; a veil covered the lower half of her face, but it was transparent and showed her features clearly. Then, with surprise, Frank saw that her jacket was made of the same material—and that she wore nothing else under it. The dark glow of her skin and darker-tipped breasts gave him a feeling of shock.

Benson ordered a bourbon and Seven-Up but Frank shook his head, and the girl moved away, her bare feet silent on the carpet. Abruptly, Frank smiled.

In a way, he thought, it was typical of the old man. The whole thing had a bizarre quality that would certainly appeal to the Hanford he remembered.

For some moments Frank had been aware of a gentle, pulsating sound. Now he realized that the lights in the room were fading slowly and that somewhere a drum was tapping—softly, gently, fading into the consciousness so that only gradually was its presence made known.

"Last show of the evening," Benson said.

The houselights were gone, and only the stage was lit. The pool at the foot of the boulders glittered like silver, as did the ring of sand, bright around it. A masculine voice, somewhere off-stage, was chanting slowly, and the keening sound of a flute joined accompaniment to his weaving, sinuous melody. The sounds were distant, vaguely heard, like the lonely ghost of a desert song.

As the theme was repeated, growing more insistent, the lights began changing color. Filtering down onto the patch of sand and water they shone first violet, then blue, then each ascending shade of the spectrum, till a clear, whitish-yellow shimmer filled the open space like liquid sunlight.

And then the music stopped.

A moment's pause—then the thud of the drum began again, more slowly, now, beating as though to measured steps.

A girl appeared at one side of the stage, tentative as a fawn at first, stepping out onto the sand, bare feet and shapely legs flashing briefly from the flowing white robe that swathed her. Her fine-featured face was lifted high, jet black hair swept up to a knot at the back of her head, then falling in a long rope down against the white cloth. The girl's face burned mahogany against the white of her garments; her high, full cheekbones and tilted eyes were exotic, native-looking, her slender neck smooth as carved teak, balanced above her straight shoulders.

Frank looked at the girl, thinking that there was something very familiar about her, the proud carriage and beautifully sculptured features—and then he looked again. And stared. Her skin was too dark, of course—probably stained for the performance— but there could be no mistaking the rest; he knew that face and the poised manner of moving too well. In fact, he was amazed, now, seeing her again, to find how perfectly he did remember Vikki!

The current of music had begun again, joining the drumbeat and flowing to a more rapid rhythm. The girl, as though assured that she was alone under the blind-starred sky, began to move more freely and, at last, to swirl in a slow dance. As she turned in sweeping patterns, the robe flared out to reveal the shape of long, tan, classically muscled legs, then fell back again, a glittering white shroud.

More and more rapidly the music wailed, and the girl gradually gave herself up to a graceful ecstasy of dancing, spinning to the increasing volume of the phrase as though the notes possessed her, commanding her liquid movements. She thrust out her arms in supplication to the lonely night, gyrating the uninhibited ritual, ever faster until—with a final whirl, the robe swept free and fluttered loosely to the ground like a broken, white bird.

The girl stood, clad only in a filmy harem costume, her dark, oiled body gleaming under the lights, incredibly sensual in its attitude of secret and mysterious abandon.

Slowly she began dancing again, wild and unashamed. Her feet struck showers of sand into the water as she moved around the perimeter of the pool, and she did things with her hands ....

There was a man walking up the aisle, looking into the seats on either side as he came. When he saw their table, he moved forward quickly. He was younger than Frank, well-built, with a square face and light blond hair. Benson, too, noticed his approach.

"Hello, Jay," he said to the newcomer.

"About time you were getting here," the other answered.

"The rain slowed us down."

"This him?"

"Yeah."

"Okay, Hanford is waiting upstairs."

Benson stood up, and Frank, reluctant to pull his eyes from the stage, followed suit. He took one last look at Vikki, marveling at the lithe savagery with which she moved to the now-frenzied music, bending backwards, the coil of ebony hair brushing the sand. Further and further she arched; corded muscles stood out sharply beneath the shining skin, lush breasts spread as she leaned still farther, the top of her head almost touching. Then the music crashed, the girl's legs folded under her, her knees struck the sand, and she lay flat on her back, arms thrown wide, chest heaving from exertion. There was an instant's pause, then she twisted to her feet again, tore away the gauzy costume with an animal cry, and leaped forward into the shining pool.

Mercifully, the lights went out.

Frank wiped the film of perspiration from his face. His brain was swept with a torrent of memories, a staggering understanding of what it might actually mean to "come back"—to be here, where she was again. Earlier, when he had thought of it, he had envisioned a stiff, uncomfortable moment of embarrassment at their meeting—then, perhaps, mutual avoidance. But now he knew—was convinced beyond reason—that it would not be that way. Not that way at all.

"Come on," Jay Ginther said, "let's go!"

They went out of the dining room, into the lobby, and then up a curved flight of stairs leading to the second floor. It was darker still on the upper story, a line of small floorlights marking one side of the hall and a low rail the other. He walked next to Benson, Ginther several paces ahead.

"Who all is here?" Frank asked.

"Guy named Joe Hines, another called 'Cat'. You don't know either of them. They've worked with Hanford a lot before, though."

"What's it all about?"

The big man glanced at him, grinned and said nothing.

They stopped at a door near the end of the passage, and Ginther pressed a button. There was an answering buzz and he pushed the door open. "Find yourselves a seat," he said, "I'll get him."

They were standing in a large room, obviously the main chamber of Hanford's personal suite. The place was brightly lit, decorated in a cold, modem style, a real contrast with the extravagance downstairs. On one wall he noticed a familiar sight: a large wooden cabinet enclosing a group of various-sized and -shaped knives—part of Hanford's collection. Like all of the old man's hobbies, the knives had a sinister aspect, for each had been originally designed for the purpose of killing one particular kind of animal—the human.

The interior furnishings were completed by a huge aquarium-tank at the far end of the room, separating identical doors— one painted black and the other white. Ginther had gone through the black door in search of their host. Frank's eyes rested on the tank of water a moment, then he turned his attention to the other occupants of the room.

There were two men present, besides himself and Benson. One was in the straight-backed chair at the far end of the room, near the aquarium. He was looking at Frank in unconcealed appraisal. He was small and delicate of build, with a distinctively Oriental-looking face. His eyes were his most arresting feature, large and direct. When Frank first looked at him, the lids slid back to reveal extremely large pupils, then narrowed to sleepy, disinterested slits. The effect was unmistakable—this was the one they called Cat.

The other man was seated in a deep, black-cushioned armchair, nonetheless managing to look tense and uncomfortable. His frame was very thin; long, sharp shoulders hunched forward, splinters of legs extended. He threw a brief glance at the two as they came in, his eyes avoiding Frank's. One of the skeletal hands lifted slightly toward them. "Hi, Arnie," he said.

"How are you, Joe," Benson answered. "Hello, Cat." The small man in the straight-backed chair moved his head in what might have been a sign of recognition.

They sat down on the large couch near the sliding doors. Frank could see dim furniture shapes outside, and, toward the far end, the frame of the night sky. He was looking out on a terrace, furnished for use as a sun-deck. A nagging thought that had occurred to him when they'd first entered the club came back strongly now—just what did Hanford want with him? It was obvious the old man was doing all right for himself—why had he been so anxious to find Frank? And why bring him here? It was useless, of course, to speculate, when he'd be having his questions answered so soon.

He grew nervous after a moment and got up to walk over to the aquarium. Curiously, he looked in through the glass; a group of reddish-black fish was swimming lazily inside. They moved as a unit—more than a dozen of them on each side of the partition which halved the tank—first sweeping toward the wall of glass, then veering away at the last instant. They were not like any species he could recall seeing before and did not seem particularly attractive. It seemed an odd exhibit.

"Don't go dangling a finger in there," Benson warned from the couch. He looked around. "Piranhas," the big man said, grinning. "Meat-eaters."

Frank had heard of such fish—bloodthirsty enough to attack a man or larger animals, equipped with powerful jaws and rows of sharp teeth; a sufficient number could strip a carcass to the bone in a matter of minutes. He looked at the evil, close-set eyes and thick bodies and shuddered slightly. He should have known—another of Hanford's macabre hobbies!

When he had first known the old man it had been lepidoptery—but not the innocent collecting and mounting of harmless bugs and butterflies. With Hanford it had to be *poisonous* insects. When it was painting, he had done watercolors of preying animals; with cooking, famous last repasts—the normal turned around, the ordinary twisted and distorted, made disgusting and a little sick.

The door on his left opened. Jay Ginther stopped, leaning against the jamb and looked around. He saw Frank by the tank and said, "Sit down."

Shelby felt a quick stab of anger, then forced it back. He was surprised how much the blond-haired man already annoyed him. Still, this was not the time to argue. He went back to the couch and sat down.

As though reading his thoughts, Benson leaned over and said quietly, "Don't sass Junior—it's not healthy."

Ginther crossed the room and took up a position near the outside door. They waited in silence, and a moment later there was a movement in the hallway behind the black door.

Stanley Hanford walked into the room.

The little man in the black alpaca-like suit might have been a preacher of the gospel. His head was large and egg-shaped, pale skin drawn tightly over the high forehead and domed pate, bald save for a thick tuft of hair that began above each ear and extended in a thin ridge around the back of his skull. His eyes were sparsely browed and lively, his nose a sharp but prominent, rather long blade, and his mouth—though wide and at the moment smiling—was somehow bloodless and potentially cruel. The first look gave the impression of a preacher, all right—but a second reminded one more of a politely smiling barracuda.

The old man advanced into the room, his quick eyes taking in everything at once, darting to each occupant in order, then settling finally on Frank. Alert head cocked slightly to one side, smile widening on his face, Hanford walked directly over to him.

"My dear boy, I'm so happy to see you again. You've arrived just in time! Now you'll be able to help us in our little project!"

Frank felt a shock of surprise. He had not expected anything this sudden. He wanted to yell *wait a minute—not so fast—I haven't agreed to anything yet*. But he had no chance. The low, reedy voice swept on, a fanatic confidence silencing all argument.

"Yes," the old man repeated, "just in time. Now we will be able to take advantage of your most remarkable talents—and in the interests of a most remarkable venture. I think you'll agree. Because you are going to have to show us how to steal a bank, my boy—not rob it, you understand—but *steal* it…. The entire bank!"

19

# CHAPTER THREE

SUPPOSE YOU'RE CURIOUS to know more about all this?"

Hanford had dismissed the others, sending them away with instructions to meet the next morning. Frank had remained behind at Hanford's request. "Let's go back into my office where we can talk."

Frank followed the small man through the black-painted door, down a narrow corridor to Hanford's personal rooms. The old man motioned him inside.

Looking around, Frank recognized certain items of bric-a-brac. These were pieces of a collection Hanford called "triggers"—objects which had caused or figured in various murders. When he could not obtain the original he had a copy made, and there were such unlikely notions as bell-cords and billiard balls, as well as paperweights, letter openers and ice-picks.

Hanford indicated the leather chair to Frank, and went around behind the desk himself. "Well, my boy, I suppose this all sounds fantastic to you, but I haven't gone batty, I assure you. I'm quite serious, and with your help I fully intend to go through with my idea. Drink?" He pulled a serving tray closer from the side of the broad walnut expanse.

Frank rubbed his cheek tiredly. "That would go all right."

"Irish and soda, if memory serves?"

Shelby nodded. When Hanford finished mixing the drink and handed his glass to him, he swallowed down half its contents in quick gulps, letting the cold, bubbling liquid help cut away the deep weariness he felt.

Hanford poured himself a small goblet of red wine and sat back to sip it appreciatively. "This is a fabulous opportunity, my boy. Yes—upon my word, it's the chance of a lifetime." Frank heard the excitement creeping into the old man's voice, watched the sanguine expression grow more vivid.

"A number of months ago I came into possession of information of a startling nature. I found that a local bank, a very large and wealthy organization, was intending to move its quarters from one section of New York to another. I was interested at once, of course. Think of it! In order to accomplish a physical move of this sort, no drafts or checks can suffice—the money itself must be taken out of the vault, transported through the city streets, and placed into a new one."

Hanford laughed with delight. "I thought to myself, Why, Stanley, it would be the most amazing thing ever dreamed of—if you could *steal a bank!* Pick it off whole!"

There could be no question—the light of fanaticism was in Hanford's face. Frank understood then. This was his "masterpiece," and he was like a child with an incredibly desirable toy in its grasp. Hope sank inside him. Reason would be powerless against this unexpected tide of pure, distilled cupidity.

"Of course, I would not have dreamed of such a feat being possible—think of the guards that will be used—had it not been for one fact. The man who came to me with the news was employed by the armored car firm most likely to be employed for the transfer! As it happened, unfortunately, a rival company was awarded the contract, but my man was still in possession of much vital information. He was a regular patron of the small gambling room I have in the back of the club, and I had spoken to him once or twice before—had the impression that he wanted somehow to call himself to my attention. He came to me with the news like a dog with a bone in his teeth. I petted him quite friendlily—" The old man chuckled—"and took the bone."

Frank finished his drink and put down the glass. "That's all very interesting," he said, "but what has it got to do with your dragging me here?"

"I told you, Frank, you're going to help us plan this job. We have information, but that's all. A master skill is required to make anything workable from it, and you have that skill—a natural flair for seeing the chink in even the best-planned armor."

"I'm sorry, Hanford," Frank said, "but you've got it wrong. I'm not going to help you." Quickly, he followed up the surprise in the old man's face. "I've built a good life for myself since I left you, and I don't plan to see it destroyed. You think you know me, but you don't—you knew someone else, someone who doesn't exist any more."

The old man was smiling ironically. "Yes, I see—in other words, the person I knew is dead now," he said. "Is that what you mean? Perhaps it will come as a surprise, but I believe you, my boy—yes, I believe what you say." Then, abruptly, he was leaning forward, his smile gone, his voice a harsh whisper. "But wouldn't it be a shame if *you* had to pay the penalty for that dead man's crimes!" he hissed. "How tragic that the police, failing to find that 'other' one, insisted that *you* were the accomplice to the killing of that warehouse guard five years ago!"

"I had nothing to do with that—you know it!"

"Yes!" Hanford was leaning back, smiling again. "I know it. And I know about that 'other' man being dead now, replaced by one who looks quite like him. Who even has the same fingerprints. That's very important knowledge, isn't it? A man must be careful what he does with such knowledge. For, you see, there are few in this world of cynics who would understand what you've just told me—most would be inclined to judge hastily. And, I'm afraid, harshly."

"You're going to turn me in? What if I decide to tell what I know?" Frank said, fighting desperately now.

"An interesting thought. What *do* you know?"

"Enough to break up your little party."

The other shook his head slowly. "I don't believe so, Frank, I really don't. If you'll think back you'll remember that all the jobs you were in on were planned very carefully—which was why you were in on them—because you were the cleverest finger-man I ever knew, my boy. I wasn't implicated, and neither were you— except for that one slip with the guard, when Ritch got trigger-happy and you were seen running out of the building. So far as the other capers were concerned, you could implicate me, Frank, but to do so you would have to name yourself as well. You would have to serve a year for every year I served."

"I've got more of them than you have, Hanford."

The small man behind the desk shook his head again. "Not to spend in prison," he said. "No one has any years to spare in prison, Frank." His smile was gentle now. "I have you, Frank—we both know it."

For one instant Frank thought he would do it—jump up from his chair and grab the little man by his lapels and march him off to the nearest cop. He'd see who stuck behind bars the longest. And then he remembered Nancy. What would be left when he got out? Everything he'd done for the past five years he'd done for her. Did it make sense to throw that all away?

"What's your deal, Hanford?"

"The simplest possible, Frank. Plan this job for me, and you are free to go—the debt is paid."

Frank grinned wryly at the word "debt" and said, "That sounds good, but how do I know you're on the level?"

"There are no assurances, my boy. None whatsoever. After all, I need none, do I? But be reasonable. As you can see, I don't really need the money from this job—though it will consolidate my holdings nicely—and I will be taking part in no more after-ward. What further use could I possibly have for you?"

Frank started to make a sneering, obvious answer, then stopped. He glanced up. There was a strange, expectant look in the old man's eyes, and suddenly he had a feeling in the pit of his stomach as though he had stepped to the edge of a bottomless chasm—and stopped in the last possible instant of time.

"All right," he said quietly. He accepted the cigarette the old man offered him. "For my own amusement, how did you find me? Sort of convenient, wasn't it, just when you needed help?"

"Not at all, in fact. You see, I've known where you were for almost a year, now."

"You what?"

"Exactly. I had a report nearly ten months ago that sounded good, and I sent Cat to verify it. You wouldn't have been aware— he posed as a security investigator checking on a mythical relative in New York."

"Then why didn't you—"

"Come after you? Hanford finished his glass of wine and put it aside, pushing the tray back on his desk. "Yes, that was my first thought, of course—to come and get you and punish you for your ingratitude, for betraying my trust."

Frank resisted an impulse to laugh—then decided it wouldn't have been a laugh, anyway.

"And then I thought, no—why do it that way? Time for that later. In the meanwhile, he may be of use." He looked up, smiling. "And, you see, I was right. We are helping each other again."

Frank nodded tiredly. It was all growing clear now.

"But you're tired, of course!" the old man said, getting up quickly. "I'm sorry to have kept you so long after your hard ride." He walked with him to the door.

"As I told the others, I like everyone to stay here at the club during the planning of a project such as this, so I'll ask you to be my guest, too." His voice was genial, he was the suave host again. They went down the corridor to the front room, Hanford showing him the way. "The others will be in rooms off the main hall, but I had hoped you would share my suite with me."

The large front apartment was empty now, the lights extinguished except for one near the door and the glow that came from the green depths of the aquarium. The latter cast an eerie gloom over the smartly furnished chamber. Hanford indicated a door leading off the big room, next to the end of the bar.

"There is a bedroom and bath through there," he said. "You may use this area for your living quarters. I never need it except on occasions like tonight."

Hanford pointed around the room. "There's the bar, a record player and radio at the far end, and you doubtless noticed the patio and sun-deck when you came in. We have a pool downstairs you may use during the day. The water's heated and quite pleasant, and there are swim things in your room. I think you'll find it all quite convenient. The room phone is connected downstairs only, by the way. You can order your meals up or eat in the dining room."

"Thanks, I'll make out."

"Good. We'll get together here in the morning and you'll meet Jim Fogherty, the man I was telling you about."

"Fine," Frank said, feeling a fresh wave of weariness settle on him.

"I'll leave you, then," Hanford said. "Good night."

"Good night," he said. The door closed and a tumbler clicked.

Frank had changed clothes for bed when he decided a drink would help unravel his nerves for sleep. Slipping a robe on, he went back into the darkened room to the bar.

A full cabinet of bottles extended along the mirrored backboard, and in the reflected light from his room he found the square bottle of Bushmill's. He decided to do without soda and poured the drink straight into a large glass, adding water from the small sink. As he turned, he heard a small noise, a stirring. His eyes traveled to the door through which Hanford had exited—it was still closed, motionless as its twin, the white one.

Then, slowly, a chill traced its way down the back of his neck and centered in his stomach. The white door was no longer white—not all of it. There was someone standing framed against it. He turned toward the figure, lowering his glass.

"Hello ... Frank," a voice said, a voice that made the sound of his heartbeat begin pounding in his ears; a voice low and controlled, as intimate from across the room as it would be next to his ear.

He cleared the tightness from his throat. "Hello, Vikki," he said. "I wondered when I'd see you."

He heard a soft laugh, and the girl moved from the door, passed in front of the dimly lighted aquarium and came toward him.

"I've been wondering the same thing," she said, "—for quite a long time." She stopped in the shaft of light from Frank's room. She was dressed in a dark-blue evening gown, bare arms and shoulders milk white, tinted with olive. The makeup from her act had been removed. She waited while he looked at her, his eyes moving obediently over the lines of her light-and-shadow loveliness—the sophisticated high cheeks and chiseled nose, the large intensity of her eyes, dark against the paleness of her face. A cascade of lustrous raven hair splashed down to her naked shoulders, framing her face and the perfect column of her neck. Her breasts, which swelled beneath the lacy evening dress, were firmly contained, drawing sharply in to a flat, narrow waist and seductively molded hips. She let him look at her fully, then moved out of the light and sat down at the bar.

He groped for words to break the silence. "It would be pretty inane of me to say you're looking good, Vikki—you're looking beautiful. More beautiful than ever."

She smiled at him. "Thank you. I think that calls for a drink." Crossing her arms on the counter-top, she watched him as he mixed Scotch and water in the proportions she liked. As he finished the drink, he searched again for words to drop into the pool of silence deepening around them. "I saw your act tonight," he said.

"Same old Victoria." She smiled. "Still with dreams of talent—at least they don't throw things. What about you, Frank? What have you been doing?"

"Working," he said, putting her glass in front of her. "Staying out of trouble."

She nodded. There was another brief pause, and then she said, "Why did you come back, Frank?"

"To do a job," he said, deciding not to lie.

"Oh. Just like that?" she asked. "You decided to come back to do a job? You must have needed the money pretty bad."

He walked around the end of the counter so that the light from his room was at his back, the glow slanting over his shoulder to illuminate Vikki's cheek and the arm nearest him. He wondered if he should try to explain, then decided not to. "There were other reasons, of course," he said.

She smiled at that and didn't answer. "Well, then," she said brightly, holding up her glass, "success!" He joined the toast with a feeling of uneasiness, not knowing how to answer. "What do you think of the place?" She made a little gesture around the room with one hand.

"Fancy."

"Not bad. Of course it isn't the Armbruster, but then—"

Surprisingly, they both laughed. The hotel she'd mentioned was the one in which Hanford had originally had his headquarters—where they had first met—a cheesy brick tenement building on the East Side. They had held their meetings and conferences—surrounded by a choice assortment of gamblers, pimps and prostitutes—in an apartment which the old man had furnished in the general style of a ladies' tea room.

"Cigarette?" He shook loose a pack and handed it to her, then held a light. She touched his hand to steady the flame. Her fingers felt cool.

"Do you stay here?" he asked.

Vikki nodded and glanced at him. "A lot of people do," she said levelly—then smiled again. "It's a nice place. Like some music?"

"Why not?"

She slid down from the stool, went to the far end of the bar and flipped a switch built into the wall. He watched her, wondering at the seeming friendliness the girl was showing. Was it genuine, or was it to cover up her true feelings about the man who had walked out on her five years before?

"You can freshen those up," she said, adjusting the knobs to a low volume of smooth music. He went behind the bar and made another drink for each of them, placing the glasses on the counter-top as the girl returned. She sipped at her drink briefly and put it down.

"Dance, bartender?" she said.

"Vikki, I—" But she came into his arms, and then they were moving, slowly, in time to the music.

This was wrong, he knew, and he should stop. Somehow, though, the relief of having the girl react so casually toward what had happened between them reassured him and made him reluctant to risk offending her. When the number was over, they sat down again.

"You know," he began, "I'm glad that—"

"That I'm not sore?" she drank, then lowered the glass and looked down into its pale contents, swirling them gently. "I guess maybe at first I was, a little. But after I had time to think it over—" She shrugged.

"It wasn't you I was running from, Vikki, it was the whole thing—my entire life till that time. I was tired and fed up and—well, a little scared too, I guess. Anyway, I had to get out. I knew it wouldn't have worked between us, so—"

"So—" She smiled at him—"that's that."

She finished the second drink in two deep swallows and stood up, stretching out her arms to him as the music from the radio began another number.

He started to say no, but a warmness from the drinks he'd had seemed to ask *why not?* and he stood up too.

The girl fit easily against him, and they danced as they had always danced, her head resting lightly on his shoulder, the curve of her bare back lithe and responsive beneath his hand. He remembered how well they danced together—better, actually, than he and Nan. He thought of Nancy, then, with sudden shame and, stopping, let his arms fall away from the girl. She looked up at him calmly, still with one hand on his shoulder, their bodies touching. With the other hand, Vikki reached up and brushed the thick fall of hair back from her cheek. Her dark, full eyes held his and her curved lips parted just slightly, showing the tips of even, white teeth between them. Then, carefully and deliberately, her upraised arm went around his neck, and he felt the pressure of her body hard against him. The moist, red lips came to meet his, and he tasted the faint raspberry of her mouth, felt the parting of her lips and quick thrust of her tiny, pointed tongue. Desire started in him like the touch of an electric current. He stiffened under the needle-bite of her nails on his neck and arms and gripped her waist with both hands.

And then she pulled away.

The girl half-turned from him, and as if in slow motion he saw her arm come around in a flat arc, felt the searing blow across his face and staggered back. The force with which she struck him and the speed with which she moved away upset his balance, and he fell against the bar-top, almost slipping to the floor.

His head sagged forward, and he paused an instant to take a full breath. Rage washed through his body as though hot acid had been shot into his veins. He whirled, nearly blind with anger and humiliation, caught the girl's arm as she raised it to strike him again and bent it in a wrenching sweep to her side. She cried out in pain and twisted against him, her body arched rigidly under the torture of his grip.

"You son of a bitch!" she said. "You low, vile, son of a bitch!" Her head was back, spitting words into his face. Amazed by the hatred there, his own anger and swept away in the flood of the girl's fury. He released his hold and let her step back. "God, how I hope you suffer," she cried, rubbing her arm. "How I hope you writhe! So, you walk back in here after five years, big and cocky, all set to pull a job'—all ready to take over where you left off!"

She was backing across the room, toward the door she had entered, and he saw that tears were glistening on her contorted face as she raged at him.

"Well, you're *not*—you're not taking over anything. And if you touch me again, he'll *kill* you!" The girl turned and ran from the room.

For a long moment, Shelby did not move. He stood, rubbing his hand along his cheek and listening to the echo of Vikki's words. At last he turned and went back into his room. He was not angry, he found, for he understood now what the girl had thought, and he couldn't blame her for reacting as she had. It was his own fault—he'd been stupid not to explain immediately. But something she'd said hung undigested in his mind as he switched out the light and got into bed—she'd said, *"he'll kill you…"*

And somehow he was certain she hadn't meant Stanley Hanford.

# CHAPTER FOUR

GOOD MORNING, FRANK!" Hanford had phoned him they were coming up, so he was not surprised to see the others waiting as he came out of his bedroom. The old man was wearing the same black suit, white shirt and high collar that he'd had on the night before, and Frank remembered that he seldom wore anything else.

"You haven't met Jim Fogherty yet," Hanford said. "Jim, this is Frank Shelby."

A large, loosely built man in a gray tweed sportcoat and open-throated shirt moved toward him. He had wide shoulders and a big, square face with Irish features. His ash-colored hair was long and combed flat at the sides, but it was thinning a bit in front and on top. He looked like an ex-fullback from the Big Ten, but one who had become a little soft and shabby. The man shoved out a wide, strong hand, and Frank shook it.

"Happy to meet you," Fogherty said, showing his white, even teeth in a laugh. Frank nodded.

"Let's all sit down," Hanford suggested. "I'm sure you're anxious to get started." Ginther remained at his post between them and the front door, but the others found chairs around the room.

"Now then, I'll begin by giving you a general idea of our project." He walked quickly over to the terrace doors, pulling the drapes shut and dropping the room into semi-darkness. He then went back to stand beside a table which Frank had not noticed previously, and upon which a motion picture projector had been set up. Hanford pressed the switch. An image sprang into focus on the far wall; they were looking at a street scene, uptown New York, apparently shot from the window of a moving car.

For a moment they watched in silence, then Hanford said, "As we pass the next comer, look to your right.... There—that building is the Wellingford Federal Bank." The camera bobbled, blurring the picture. "You'll see we've turned south, headed downtown now."

The unsteady image fluttered against Frank's eyes, flickering and jerking until the frames seemed to spin inside his brain, beating a steady tattoo against the optic nerves. He forced himself to look, watching the numbered streets go by—96th, 79th, 60th—seeing the familiar flow of traffic in both directions, the heavy throngs of people on the sidewalks. Several times the car stopped for a signal and then moved on again.

"Here you'll see us turn on fifty-fifth," Hanford said, and a moment later, "There it is—the new home of the Wellingford!"

This was the transfer route, then. Frank pursed his lips. Watching the scenery on both sides of the street as it fell behind the camera, he had seen nothing to give him the slightest ray of hope. Like a doomed man, he waited for Hanford to switch the lights back on and return to his chair.

"You will notice," the old man said, "that the distance traveled was quite short—three and three-tenths miles, to be exact, I believe, Jim?"

Fogherty nodded.

"At fifteen miles per hour, that's a bit over ten minutes travel time. In just a few days the Wellingford will move, taking the route we've just seen. They will travel at night, under a heavy guard. With them will be the company's entire assets, negotiable and otherwise. The cash and currency should be in the near vicinity of twenty million dollars. That's what we're after."

There was a flat silence in the room, broken only by someone's breathing. Frank waited to hear a protest. No one moved.

"Look," he said at last, "every cop in New York will be on that convoy, and it's right in the middle of town. Hell, it'd take a division of infantry to crack it."

"Jim, here, can tell us exactly what the guard arrangements are."

Fogherty hunched forward. "Well, the O'Farrell Company got the bid—they're an armored car outfit, and they have a private guard service, too. There'll be cops, of course, but O'Farrell is running the show."

"That's not your company?"

"No, mine's Van Ness. We missed out. But a lot of guys at our place know guys at O'Farrell—this friend of mine and I, we've talked about it a lot, so I know most of what's going on."

"I see."

"There'll be a crew at either end of the switch," Fogherty continued, "since they figure trouble is most likely during loading or unloading, before the dough is actually locked inside the trucks. Then there'll be a half-dozen motorcycle cops as escort, at least one cruiser, and extra guards in each of the four trucks. That includes driver, shotgun messenger and enclosed rear guard. The 'messenger' has a sub-machine gun."

"How many people will we be working with?" Frank asked Hanford.

"Everyone you see here," the old man answered.

"What?"

"I don't want a lot of extra people on this job, Frank," Hanford said.

"But this is crazy!" He looked around quickly. "Five men—six, if you're in—against a set-up like the one he's talking about?"

The old man nodded.

He wanted to stand up and start yelling—pound on the small man and force him to understand what he was suggesting. He wanted to shout to the others that they were fools not to see that this thing couldn't be done—not by *four* gangs the size of theirs.

Instead, he sat numbly in his chair, thinking what it would mean if he failed now to do the obviously impossible.

"How much time?" he mumbled stupidly after a moment.

"Ten days," Fogherty told him. "The movement is next Friday night."

"Ten days…"

Fogherty went on: "Another neat trick is that they've got the trucks rigged with police wave-length radios, right on one of the dispatch bands, so anything that happens is reported into the general broadcast pattern. You see, they're on a timetable every foot of the way, including traffic signals and all, so if they get more than sixty seconds behind the alarm goes, and they close in on the area."

Perspiration beaded Frank's upper lip, causing a mild tickling sensation. He did not wipe it off. He stared at Jim Fogherty.

"My friend at O'Farrell says they'll close off the side streets about an hour before, keep all traffic—even pedestrians—out until the convoy goes past."

Shelby did stand up then, brushing against an ashtray and sending it toppling to the floor. He didn't look down at the ashtray, he stared only at the two men. "You're both crazy," he said and walked across to the bar. It was early, but he mixed himself a drink. A strong one.

Hanford followed him over. "Frank, now I know it sounds difficult—"

"*Difficult!*" he cried, whirling back to face Hanford. "This is the craziest, most outlandish—"

"—but you'll think about it for a while, and I'm sure it won't look so impossible to you later. Don't forget, you haven't examined any of the details, and you often used to say that even the best of them forget something, somewhere, every time. As soon as you start looking, I think you'll enjoy the challenge."

He couldn't help it—he started laughing. The whole ludicrous business exploded over him like a wonderfully funny joke—one

34

where everybody goes around with a perfectly straight face, not letting on, but building one ridiculous and impossible premise on top of another, until the whole gimcrack structure topples down amid shouts of glee. It was pricelessly funny, a madman's dream of glory—stick up Fort Knox; kidnap King Saud; raid the Tower of London for the crown jewels. Frank roared his helpless, confused laughter into the room.

Hanford smiled uncertainly; one or two of the others chuckled, then became uneasy and silent. The sight of them staring brought still greater torrents spilling from his mouth until at last, body aching, throat dry, he felt the stream of hysterical mirth run out, and he stopped abruptly. He sagged weakly onto a bar stool and wiped at his wet eyes; the strength was gone out of him, and he was limp and defeated. Hanford's disapproving gaze held steady, a little angry and puzzled.

"You think about it," the old man repeated.

"That's right," Frank answered, tired now, "I'll think about it."

Hanford nodded. "Good. That'll be all, then. You and Jim will go into town this afternoon and drive over the route yourselves. That'll give the two of you a chance to talk some more, and you'll probably have a lot of questions to ask. Is there anything else?"

The others stood up and began moving toward the door. "Just a minute," Frank said. They stopped.

"There's just one thing I want to tell each of you. If we're going to actually try this stunt, then we're going to do it my way. I'm going to try to figure something out—what I'll come up with, I don't know. Nothing, probably. But if we do it, we'll do it clean—nobody gets hurt, is that clear?" He turned to Hanford who was watching him narrowly. "It's that way or you can count me out-regardless of anything else."

If the old man was displeased at Frank's outbreak he gave no sign. He scratched the side of his nose with one slender finger. "That after all is up to you, isn't it, Frank?" he said. "If you can work it out, fine. If not—"

Shelby didn't have to ask what he meant. He knew only too well. "That's all, then," he said, and the other men left.

Hanford hesitated at the door. "When you and Jim go into town," he said, "I trust you'll be very careful about doing anything foolish?"

He returned the old man's look. "I stick to my deals, Hanford—I hope you can say as much."

Jim Fogherty drove the late model Ford coupe past the O'Farrell Armored Transport Company for the second time, taking a right at the signal and heading downtown. He held the wheel loosely in his big hands, driving with easy confidence, ignoring the traffic around him. Frank winced frequently as they brushed by passing vehicles.

"What was the time on that run?" Fogherty asked.

Frank checked the stopwatch in his hand. "Thirteen minutes and forty seconds."

"Traffic's still pretty heavy."

"The signals are set, and we only missed one. That should get them there in a little under or over twelve even." They were not checking the transfer route itself yet, but were following the course the trucks were most likely to choose to reach the old Wellingford after leaving their dispatching office.

"Tell me how you think the trucks will be set up."

"Sure," Fogherty said. "Like I mentioned, there'll be four, total. Three men in each: driver, rear-guard and 'messenger.' The coin will be pretty evenly split up between them, because it weighs so much, but the paper stuff, like bonds and securities, will be kept separate. One truck will have currency, another paper stuff, and one of them safe-deposits."

"How will we know which one has the currency?"

"Well, the stuff is kept in different vaults at the bank, so the drivers will know which they'll be carrying by who they've been assigned to at the loading end."

"I see."

"That's about it," said Fogherty. "All the trucks go together, load at the same time. The driver and 'messenger' watch the truck, the rear-guard walks with the guys from the bank who'll actually cart the stuff outside."

"Do the trucks stop anywhere on the way to the old Wellingford Building?"

Fogherty shook his head. "No, strictly against regulations. They'll drive straight there from the dispatcher."

Frank nodded. That made it tougher.

They passed the Wellingford, a large, slate-gray building, nearly black from the years' accumulated grime. It looked small and antique, surrounded by newer, finer structures. They turned past the bank and onto the transfer route. Frank said, "Take it as slow as you can from here on."

They drove the slightly more than three-mile path a half-dozen times in steady succession. Frank made notes in a small pad as they went the first two times, then sat wordlessly watching the rest of the trips. It was much as they'd seen in Hanford's films, and his worst fears were confirmed—there were no helps of any kind—no bridges, rail-crossings, sidings, tunnels or obstructions. There was no road work going on. Just ordinary downtown streets, filled now with the ordinary amount of traffic, lined with the usual assortment of store-fronts, movie houses, restaurants, parking lots, and—

"Let's swing back over it once again," Frank said, sitting up suddenly.

Fogherty looked at him. "Got something?"

"I don't know."

They drove back over the same streets, and Frank checked both sides of the pavement carefully, making scribbled entries in his notebook. Fogherty leaned over to see what he was writing, and the car wavered halfway into the next lane. A horn sounded.

"Watch where you're going!" Frank said.

"Okay, okay." The big man laughed. He pulled back to his own side of the street and returned the horn blast. "What's that address?"

Frank looked up, staring at the other man hard until he looked away again. "Let's get back," he said coldly. But he knew he was barely concealing his excitement. It was a simple thing that had caught his attention—maybe too simple—still, if they could get hold of the right kind of equipment ...

Fogherty turned north, swinging down to the parkway and heading out of the city. After a while the big man glanced over again and said, "Mind if we stop at my place on the way? Like to pick up some things and tell the wife where I'm going."

Frank was only half listening, his mind still eagerly exploring the discovery he'd made. "What?" he said. "How long?"

"Just a couple of minutes."

"I don't want to get back late." The reference to a home and wife surprised him; he had not considered Fogherty as a married man.

"We'll hurry," the other assured him.

Fogherty's house was small, a domestic-looking frame bungalow situated in a typical suburban neighborhood north of the city. The grass and low hedges were neatly trimmed, and a curved walk edged with flowers led up to the front porch.

"Come on in a minute?"

Frank shook his head. "I'll wait here."

"Come on, Sandy would like to meet you." Was that the note of the proud husband in Fogherty's voice? Frank looked at the man with new interest. Partly from curiosity, he got out of the car and went up to the house. The door was opened by a small, modestly pretty girl with freckles and reddish-brown hair.

"Hello, Jim," the girl said, smiling at him, then at Frank.

"Hi, honey, meet Frank Shelby, friend of Mr. Hanford's. We've been downtown this afternoon."

"Won't you come in?" she said.

"Well, just while Jim gets his things," he told her.

The house was clean and inexpensively furnished. There was a medium-sized living room and semi-dining area, separated from the kitchen by a serving-ledge. To the far right a door opened onto a short hallway. Frank could see several toys scattered near the entrance to the hall.

The place looked about as much like the home of a potential bank robber as a canary cage looks like an eagle's nest. He stared at Sandy and thought, I'll bet you belong to the P.T.A.—and I'll bet you think your husband spends his spare time playing poker with the boys. ...

"Excuse me while I change, Frank," the big man said and went down the hallway.

"Can I get you a cup of coffee, Mr. Shelby?"

He sat down in a large overstuffed chair, faded and rather out of date, showing the effects of hard use. He watched the girl Sandy putting on a pan of water to heat and taking down a jar of instant coffee. She was quite young, an easy-smiling, Irish sort of a girl.

"Black, Mr. Shelby?"

"Please, and make that Frank, would you?"

She came out of the kitchen with a steaming cup in each hand. "All right, Frank," she said. "Here you are. Jim likes his with lots of cream and so much sugar it makes me dizzy just to put it in. I make him do it." She put the other cup down on a tray with a sugar and creamer on it, then sat across from him. "You work for Mr. Hanford?" she said.

He hesitated, then nodded.

"I've never met him, but Jim has told me he's very important."

"He's quite, uh, influential," Frank said, beginning to feel strangely uncomfortable. From the back of the house he could hear Fogherty humming loudly to himself.

"This is rather a special assignment you're on now, isn't it?" the girl asked.

Damn Fogherty for taking so long. What was he trying to do to him? He didn't know what the man had told his wife. "Well, I guess you could say it's a little unusual," he said.

"How's that?"

"Well, it's—it's quite large, for one thing."

The girl was leaning slightly toward him now, her eyes serious, her voice cast a shade lower. "Do you think it's—dangerous?"

He held his breath, looking at her. No, she didn't know. But she was guessing and trying hard to get him to let something slip. Frank opened his mouth to say "No," but he saw the girl's eyes, full on him, pleading, and the word hung in his throat.

"Then it is," she said.

"No, that is—Please, Sandy, I don't—"

The sound of Fogherty's humming came closer, and the big man appeared in the doorway. Frank stood up quickly.

"Sorry to hold things up. Honey, I'll call you in the morning and tell you just how long we'll be. A couple of days, I guess, maybe more."

The girl walked with them to the door. "Don't you have time for your coffee, darling?" she asked.

"Uh-uh, better not. Frank's due back, and besides, they've got plenty at the restaurant." He held the small girl by the shoulders and kissed her with genuine feeling. "You be good now, and tell Katie I'll be seeing her real soon."

Frank listened to their good-bys, not wanting to, but caught inside the door by Fogherty's large bulk. When the big man stepped past him and down the stairs, Frank followed. He did not look at the girl as he passed. "Good-by," he said, "glad to have met you."

He heard only one word as he went down the steps toward the waiting car.

"Please!" the girl whispered.

It was dark when they arrived back at the club, and Frank went up to his room, trying not to think of the scene he'd just been through. That's all you need, Shelby, he told himself. One more lost soul to worry about.

Still, something about the girl, soft and pleading, made him wish he could help Fogherty—get him out of the deal, as she had so clearly asked him to do. He had another reason for wishing the big man gone—Jim was obviously weak, a man who would not hold up under pressure, and, as such, a danger to them all. But there was nothing to be done about it. Fogherty and the information he possessed were vital to Hanford. He would remain.

Frank threw his coat down and crossed to the bar. He fixed a drink and carried it back to the couch, flicking on the light and sitting down. Strange fragments and details coursed through his mind in crazy progression, spinning it like a windmill—the likelihood of Fogherty's cracking, the questions the girl had asked him, the discovery he'd made while they were in the city, the fresh-starting hope he now felt about plotting the robbery. He could hold onto none of them long enough to make sense of any; he closed his eyes, rubbing his fingers wearily over them, streaks of light expanding like white fluff behind the closed lids.

When he opened them again, the white fluff was still there, floating before him. He focused his vision. A piece of folded paper that he hadn't seen before lay on the seat of the chair across from where he sat. He picked it up and opened the note on his knee. Four lines of slim, orderly handwriting traced across the page.

"*Frank,*" the message read. "*I am sorry about last night. I must see you. Leave the door to the terrace unlocked.*"

It was signed, "*Vikki.*"

# CHAPTER FIVE

F RANK SNAPPED THE END off his yellow pencil, cursed and
pushed a mound of loose papers away. Then he smiled
thoughtfully, got up and turned out the light over his desk. He
went out into the large, modern living room, glanced at the doors
to the terrace—then at his watch. It was late, 11:30, and Vikki had
not yet come. He had lost sense of the movement of time in the
hours just past, writing copious notes triggered by what he'd seen
in the car that afternoon. He knew now, with an exciting feeling
of relief, that he had a chance to crack it after all.

Now, the flow of ideas safely inscribed on the sheaf of papers
in his room, Frank felt washed out and very tired. He wished
he could turn in but thought of Vikki's message, and knew he'd
better not. He wondered, for the dozenth time that evening, what
she wanted to see him about. She'd made it perfectly clear how
she felt before—was tonight to rub it in or ... ?

He shrugged. Perhaps some night air would help keep his
eyes open long enough to find out the answers.

He went across to the sliding doors onto the patio, pushed
one open and stepped outside. A cool wind washed his face,
making him realize how warm it had been inside. Immediately,
he felt better. The moon was climbing whitely over the roof of the
building around the terrace, glancing off the colored flagstones
in a broken streak. He stood, gazing up at the clear sky, com-
paring it in his mind to the sky in Blaine. It looked illogically
different.

"Frank?"

Vikki, her lush figure cloaked in shadow, stood at one corner of the patio. As he watched, she stepped toward him, into the cold glow of the moon. She was clad in white toreador pants with a black, almost invisible, jersey sweater.

"You're kind of late."

She glanced behind her, walking to where he stood and stopped very close to him. "I—I thought it would be less obvious."

"Somebody minds?"

She looked past him. "Can we go inside?"

"Sure." He followed her into the room, closed the door and pulled the drapes together. Nothing of her previous anger remained, he noticed. She seemed disturbed, however, and almost fearful.

As he turned back to the room, she was taking a cigarette from the box on the coffee table, searching for a match. He walked over and held out his lighter. She drew against the bright spark, exhaled in a quick puff and let her eyes slant upwards at him.

"I—I just wanted to tell you," she said, "that I'm sorry about last night."

"Oh?"

She nodded. "I acted like a fool," she said. "I didn't know that—Well, I thought—"

"You thought that I'd just decided to come wagging my tail back to Hanford and that I expected you to be waiting with open arms."

"Yes," she said, "something like that. It was stupid of me, I know."

"And when did you find out different?"

"Today. Stanley told me. They forced you. You didn't want to come, did you?"

He shrugged. "Nobody stuck a gun in my back."

"Well—I wanted you to know, it was wrong of me," she said uncertainly.

He realized he had answered shortly. His voice was softer as he said, "That's all right, Vikki. I understood."

The girl smiled and seemed ready to leave. She hesitated, though, and he suddenly had the feeling she had come for some other reason. As though she wanted to say something else.

"Sit down a minute, if you like," he said, motioning to the couch.

"Oh, I'm probably keeping you from working."

"No," he said, surprised that she should know what he'd been doing. "As a matter of fact, I finished earlier."

Vikki's eyes widened. "Already?" she said.

"Well, there are some details to be seen to, but if nothing unexpected crops up I think I have it worked out."

"My, but you haven't lost your touch, have you?" she said and laughed, a low, pleasant sound that he had not heard since seeing her again. "That's wonderful."

He smiled at this. "There are people who wouldn't think so," he said dryly.

She seemed suddenly serious. "Will it be—dangerous?"

He felt a vague disturbance—these were very nearly the same words Sandy had spoken earlier in the day. After a moment he nodded. "Yes, as a matter of fact, I guess it will be a little touchy."

"What will you do—afterward?"

"I'll be going home, Vikki," he said. "I'll be out of here the minute it's over."

"I see," she said. There was another silence, and again Frank had the feeling that there was no reason for her not to go—unless she had something to tell him. Somehow, he knew not to ask what it was.

"Could I have a drink?" the girl asked suddenly.

Frank nodded and stood up. "Sure." He went over to the bar. A moment later, Vikki followed and sat down on one of the stools, putting her ashtray beside her.

"You're married now?"

"Yep."

"A nice girl?"

"The best," Frank said. "Her name is Nancy. You'd like her, I think."

"I know I would," Vikki answered. She took the glass he handed her and sipped from it. "Perfect," she nodded, then put the glass down and slipped lightly off the stool. "Some music?"

"Well, I don't know. Last time—"

The girl actually flushed. "I'm sorry," she said quietly. "I thought—"

At once he felt harsh and guilty. "Okay," he said, "you were right. It would be nice—why don't you get something?"

She looked at him doubtfully.

"I mean it." He smiled. "Go ahead."

She went over to the set, moving with the same sinuous grace that had distinguished her performance on the stage the night before. She was more than just a girl with a fine body and face to match. Frank watched her, remembering that she had once wanted to try acting, and thinking that girls with a lot less to offer had succeeded. She had an unselfconscious way of carrying herself, a simplicity of motion that was strangely appealing. Frank looked away, frowning. He picked up their drinks and carried them back to the couch as soft music began filtering through the room.

"How long have you been here?" he asked. Vikki came back and sat down at one end of the couch, her feet under her, the white pants outlining her curving thighs in sharp contrast against the black fabric.

"About two years—ever since Stanley had the place built."

"Nice layout." He watched the girl turn her glass nervously, not listening to him, her forehead wrinkled in thought. She drank quickly from the glass, then stood up.

"You aren't angry at me now?" she said, putting her drink on the coffee table.

He shook his head. "No," he said, "I'm not."

"Dance with me, then."

Uncertainly, Frank got to his feet. "I have no objections," he said carefully, "but I'd kind of like to know what this is all about."

The girl came close to him. "It's not 'about' anything, Frank. I'd like to forget what has happened. I'd like to forget, just for a moment, that you've been gone." Her voice was low and very soft. "I'd just like you to dance with me."

He felt her come against him, seeming smaller than life, somehow, in the tight-fitting clothes. She was warm and yielding, moving with him in slow rhythm to the music.

"It's been a long time."

She tilted her head up. "You were always good at this," she said. "You were good at everything."

They circled the room, moving in and out of the light of the single lamp near the couch. As they danced, he felt Vikki clinging closely to him, her hair near his cheek. He began to remember how it had been, a long time ago—how they had danced alone like this, letting the sweet pain of desire build inside them, their passion fanned by the veiled, implicit promise of their dancing. Her body brushed against his now, the gentle pressure of her thighs increased. He felt an excitement growing, aware that this was deliberately planned, yet he was unwilling to stop. There had been, the other times, an odor of danger about their relationship—a sitting on a powder keg that was more physical than anything else—which had somehow heightened rather than lessened their affair while it had lasted. He did not love Vikki— he later realized he never had. But the powder keg was still there, and the fuse was still quietly smoldering.

With a tremendous effort, Frank pushed himself back from the girl. She raised her head slowly and looked at him as they stopped dancing.

"What is it?"

"Let's talk for a minute," he said, controlling his voice.

She moved one hand up his shoulder till cool fingertips brushed his neck. "Can't we talk and dance?"

"Look, Vikki," he said, "I'm glad you came tonight, but to be honest, I'm wondering just why."

"Do I need a reason?"

"You don't, but I thought maybe you had one anyway."

She slipped her other arm around him and raised up on her toes. She kissed him on the mouth, hard, then moved her hand back and looked at him with a half-smile. "Maybe I do," she said.

He hesitated a moment, hating to do it, knowing he had to find out what it was she knew, what she had to tell him. Then he said, "You didn't have to come up here if that's all you wanted, Vikki—you've got other sources for that now."

She stepped back as though he had struck her across the face; her eyes widened, then narrowed, and her mouth formed a crimson snarl. "*You*—" she whispered, poised and tense. Then she whirled and started for the door. He stopped her with a name— and she turned slowly to face him.

"It is Ginther, isn't it?" he said.

Surprised he saw the anger drain from her face, leaving something akin to fear in its place. She sagged sideways onto the couch, leaning forward on both hands, her hair falling around her face.

Frank crossed the floor and sat next to her. He had to find out, and now was the time. Deftly, he forced his advantage. "What would he do if he knew you were here, with me?" he asked.

Her eyes came up to meet his. "He—he'd kill you," she said and added so softly he almost failed to hear, "He said he would."

Frank nodded. "And that's what you wanted, isn't it? That's why you came tonight—so he'd find out and even the score for what I did to you?"

She stared at him with horror, a faint groan escaping her lips. "Oh, God, Frank, how could—Oh, no, *no*—don't you under-stand? I need your help, Frank, I *hate* this place. I want you to take me with you when you go. I want to escape, and you've got to help me—please, darling, *please!*" She slipped forward, burying her face as sobs shook her body.

He stared with disbelief. He had been so sure, so positive that her hate for him had been behind her visit, that she had planned to destroy him with the blondhaired thug's jealousy. He felt nerveless and shaken at the turn of events. He felt anger, too.

"Is that why you came here? I mean, did you think I wouldn't help you unless—unless you—"

Again a despairing moan, sharper this time, and the girl pulled herself up. He moved quickly as she started to rise, catching her across the waist with one hand.

"Wait—"

"*Damn you, damn you!*" she cried, struggling to pull away; the hard muscles of her stomach strained against his hand like angry snakes beneath the thin jersey sweater.

He held on, and she turned and fought him then, fiercely, nails slashing at his face, strong body arched rigidly against his grip. He tried to keep a grip on Vikki and quiet her so that he could tell her it was all right, that he would help. But as she tore at him, he felt his own temper flooding up; as her fingers raked the side of his neck painfully, fury burst in him. He caught her shoulders, driving them against the back of the couch and pinning them there.

Her chest heaved convulsively as she lay still a moment, gasping for breath, and he saw the hatred boiling in her eyes—hatred and something else. Deliberately, she took her lower lip between small, white teeth and bit down. As a thin line of blood started she made a quick motion under him. Some pre-sense warned him, and as the slim, white-clad knee drove up swiftly for his groin he turned his hip into it and felt the painful jar of bone against tender flesh. Blind rage exploded across his brain, and he swung the girl savagely to one side, fingers hooking in the sheer jersey. A wide band of the material pulled away in his grip, baring her body from neck to waist, freeing one naked breast. Jerked off balance by the shift of weight, he fell forward, his hand covering the soft mound of flesh. With surprise and sudden understanding he felt the raised hardness of the nipple between his fingers, turned his head as her hand locked behind his neck and tasted the salt-sting of blood as their mouths met. They lay nearly still a long moment, each small movement perfect and sweet, until at last one of them reached up to touch the lampswitch. The room dropped into darkness ....

When she had gone, he lay still in the darkness. His thoughts swam slowly through the warm satiety that filled him like remembered sadness. Only gradually did he become aware of a sense of oppression at what had happened. For an instant when he had sat up, following the departing girl with his eyes across the terrace, he had thought he'd seen something else outside. But he watched a while and decided his imagination was overwrought and, with a heavy sigh, leaned back and lapsed into thick, depressing thought. Vikki needed help, but Ginther would kill him for giving it.

Wearily, he got up and walked across to the glass doors. He slid them shut and snapped the lock. As he started to turn, a glint of light caught his eye and he whirled quickly back—it was gone. He stood watching a while longer, then slowly, thoughtfully, pulled the drapes closed again. He went back to his room, stripped out of his clothes and got into bed, still thinking about what he thought he had seen. It could have been anything, of course, the moonlight on the terrace playing tricks, a window across the way. But for a moment it had not looked like a trick of his eyes; it had looked like a man's head.

Blond hair, reflecting the moonlight.

# CHAPTER SIX

T HE MAN WITH THE KNIFE did not see the door open behind
him, nor the figure of the girl as she paused and raised
a gun. There was a clicking, whirring sound, and the man
turned round. The girl fired—ten times, tiny popping sounds,
and the man fell. Stanley Hanford chuckled with glee and
turned away.

"Swiss made," he said, as the complicated clock above his
desk finished marking the hour. "An interesting variation,
wouldn't you say?"

Frank shook his head with a wry smile. "I hate to seem old
fashioned, but I always kind of liked the plain cuckoo clock."

"I'm having one made now that represents the French revolu-
tion, complete with tumbrel and guillotine!"

"Sounds great, but how about one with you coming out of
the door? You could make it sort of autobiographical—draw on
your own experience in the business."

Hanford frowned. "Your humor has become very caustic of
late, Frank. I can't say that I care much for it."

"Sorry." He suddenly felt better, glad to have scored. It made
up for having been summoned so pre-emptorily a few minutes
before to this morning's meeting. Cat and Joe Hines were already
seated when he came in, Jim Fogherty nervously pacing the floor.
They were waiting now for Ginther and Arnie to arrive.

"I must admit," the old man said, apparently mollified by the
thought, "that you have worked with incredible speed if you have
the plan completed already."

Frank nodded. The announcement that he was ready to discuss his idea for the holdup had struck wonder into the group. The advantage could swing to him now if he handled things right; he could gain the whip hand so necessary to any ideas he might get for escaping, later on.

"It isn't all worked out, you understand. There are quite a few question marks yet."

A brief knock sounded at the door, and the other two men came into the room. Frank had placed himself so that he could watch Ginther as he entered, wanting to observe any possible reaction. He also wanted to give less view of the angry red marks on the side of his neck. The younger man did not seem to notice him at all.

Hanford seemed about to call them to order, so Frank said, "All right, I'm going to go over the main outline of the plan briefly, just so I can get a couple of answers to begin with." He noticed with satisfaction that attention swung immediately to him. He was in command now, if he could hold them.

"The first point is that we're not going to try for the whole convoy—just one truck out of it. We'll take the one that has the heavy currency and let the others go."

Fogherty said, "How are you going to do that? We'll have to fight the whole convoy anyway."

"We aren't going to 'fight' anybody—in fact, there isn't going to be any shooting if I can help it. And we're taking just one truck." He stared up at the big man till Fogherty looked away. There was agitation in the heavy-featured face.

"Now, I've worked it out so that we'll have about ten or fifteen minutes to complete our job and get out of the neighborhood, so that means everybody has got to have his duty rehearsed to perfection."

This time it was Hanford himself who interrupted. "Frank, just a minute. If I remember correctly, the whole transfer—from the time the convoy leaves the old location till it arrives at the new—takes only about twelve minutes. According to Jim, even a short delay will sound the alarm, yet you say we'll have fifteen minutes to complete the holdup!"

"That's right!" Fogherty burst out. "One minute late and all hell comes at us!"

"Not if I have this thing figured right," Frank said calmly. He was not surprised to see the fear in Jim, but he marveled that the others seemed to be taking it so well. Apparently Hanford had done a good selling job on them, and they actually believed in Frank—either that or the old man had enough on each of them that they had no choice in the matter.

"As I say," he went on, "we should have at least fifteen minutes, maybe more. That will give us enough head start to move the truck out of the search area, to a place where we can unload it in peace." He glanced at the others. "How does that sound?"

"It sounds nuts," growled Benson.

Fogherty nodded, wiping his perspiring face. "You can't do something like this, Shelby. You don't realize what you're up against."

"Yessir, it sounds nuts," Big Arnie repeated, "just like all Frank's ideas used to—only thing is, they always worked." He laughed quietly.

Hanford made a small gesture with his hand. "Very well, then. What next?"

"I have some things written down here. Everyone will have to take a hand in the preparations, and they're going to cost somebody some money."

Hanford frowned. "How much?"

"Everything included will run you about twenty thousand dollars."

"*What?*"

"Here's the list," Frank said, shoving a slip of paper into Hanford's hand. The old man stared at it dumbly, finally shook his head. "But this is out of the question, Frank."

Shelby shrugged. "You're calling it—the job can't be done without the stuff I've put down there, just the way you see it."

Hanford glared unhappily at the list for a moment. Then a small smile drew at the corners of his lips. "At least I see how you plan to move the armored car," he murmured. "All right," he said suddenly. "I trust you, Frank."

Shelby nodded.

"These engines—won't they take a lot of time?" Hanford asked.

"They can be bought already fixed. Installation can be done in a day. There may be some testing and adjusting involved, though, so it would be smart to move on it today. Anyone here know cars?"

The old man gestured at Cat. "He's our mechanic, he'll take charge of that end. Arnie can help. What else?"

"Fogherty?" Frank said. The big man started visibly. "You can get a uniform that'll fit me from your outfit, can't you?"

"From Van Ness, you mean?"

"That's right."

"Well, sure, I guess, but what good's that going to do? O'Farrell is handling the job, and I can't get at one of their rigs."

"Make sure it fits," Frank said ignoring the question. "I'm six-one, a hundred and eighty-five—got that?" The other man nodded, worriedly.

"The last thing I'll need are some topographical maps and aerial views of the city, from Long Island west as far as Jersey. Also half a dozen plain city street maps."

"Joe can take care of that for you," Hanford said, "he can get them from the city."

"Fine. Then that'll do it for now."

"How about guns?" It was Ginther. "Or are we supposed to tackle a lot of choppers and automatics with squirt-shooters?"

Frank looked over toward the blond-haired man; there was nothing in the surly face but an impatient waiting for the answer to his question. "Pistols are all that will be needed, and not everyone will need those."

Ginther smiled thinly. "I'll be one of them that needs one," he said.

Frank nodded. "Yes, I can see that." The young man stared at him—his eyes made Frank uncomfortable.

"All right, then," Hanford said. "We all know what to do for now. Let's get started, and report back to me." The others stood and moved from the room.

They sat in Hanford's office, Frank in the same chair he'd had before when they'd had their first talk. The old man lighted an imported cigarette, heavily perfumed, and beamed across at him.

"Frank, I can't tell you how pleased I am at the job you're doing. Magnificient!"

"You hope."

The old man smiled. "I *know*—I remember well how you are when you set your mind to a thing."

"Hanford, let's get this straight from the start. When you told me about the deal I said it was impossible. As far as I'm concerned, it still is."

The other man looked puzzled. "But you said—"

"I said I'd work out a plan to make the hit, and I have. It's got a little better chance than if you walked up to the trucks and asked for the money—but not much. It requires a lot of luck, and a lot more and better men than you've got working for you right now."

"You underestimate the lads, my boy. They are really quite proficient."

"All right. I just wanted you to know how things stand."

"I'm certain you'll get the kinks worked out of everything by the time we go. The progress you've made already proves it."

Hanford shuffled through some notes on his desk, selected one from the pile and turned it over slowly in his hands. He seemed to pause, almost reluctant to speak again, and when he finally did his voice was overly casual.

"Incidentally, Frank, I was wondering what further part you were intending for Jim to play?"

"Fogherty? Nothing special. He'll come in handy, of course, with no more people than we've got." He did not want to express his fear of Fogherty to the old man, or admit that he had himself been wondering and worrying about just this. "Why do you ask?"

"Well, you see, Frank—" Hanford's voice fell to a confidential whisper—"I'm not too certain we can trust Jim, if you understand. To keep his head, that is." He slid another cigarette out of a little wooden box and began rolling it between his fingers, not attempting to light it. "For instance, a few minutes ago, during our meeting. I almost had the feeling he was surprised we had come this far and that we were still going ahead with the idea."

"Okay, so he's a little nervous, what's the point?" Even as Frank asked, apprehension jabbed at him. Hanford paused to touch a lighter to his cigarette, inhaled once and released a shaft of dissolving smoke through his pursed lips.

"The point is, Frank, I don't want anything to go wrong—for all our sakes. We can't afford to let Jim cause us any trouble."

"Send him away."

Hanford chuckled. "Don't be foolish, my boy. Jim is the one who brought me this idea to begin with. We can't cut him out— he wouldn't stand for it, he'd betray us in an instant."

"Then leave him in, but don't take him on the job."

Hanford shook his head. "No, that won't work either. Jim is scared. He's going to crack soon, and the only way we can protect ourselves is to get rid of him. I have decided he must be disposed of, Frank."

"No dice, Hanford," Frank said sharply. "I told you to start with that I wouldn't work if anyone was going to get hurt. That still goes."

"You were referring to the policemen and guards," the old man said. "This is different."

"I was referring to anybody!"

Hanford frowned and studied him. "I must say you seem very concerned about our friend Mr. Fogherty."

"No, no, you don't get it—I'm not concerned about anybody in the rotten bunch but me," Frank snapped. "And to me that means no killing—*none.* Or I'm out."

"I'm afraid that getting out of this is not going to be easy, Frank."

"That cuts two ways, it won't be easy for either of us."

"And what will your wife think when she learns the truth about you?"

"I'm glad you asked that," Frank said levelly. "That's a good point. I've thought about it a lot. You see, there won't be anybody waiting for me when I get out, if anything happens. You have to remember that Nancy comes from one of the town's old and respectable families; her old man would have our marriage annulled before the ink was dry on my verdict."

Frank stood up.

"That's why if I walk out you aren't going to do anything about it—because you know that if I lose, I lose everything and I won't hesitate to take you with me. So think it over. No killings, or no Frank Shelby."

The old man glared up at him silently. "You're making a mistake, Frank."

"Maybe. What about Fogherty?"

"I wouldn't risk the job with him around," Hanford said. He smiled a little. "And I wouldn't miss this job for any consideration. So I guess that's your answer, Frank."

The younger man shrugged. "You're the boss, but my stand doesn't change. The minute you dump Fogherty I'm through. And that's final. Don't say I didn't warn you." He turned and walked to the door. He opened it, then looked back at the old man sitting thoughtfully in his chair.

"Maybe you've got a bad deal with Jim," Frank said, "but remember that without me you've got no deal at all."

He closed the door as he went out.

Once back in his own room, Frank began to think fast. He didn't know what Hanford would do now, but whatever it was wouldn't be pretty. He'd seen the old man when he was crossed before. One thing was clear—he had to get out.

He picked up the phone and clicked the receiver. "Miss Porter, please," he said when the man named Pete answered. The phone in her room rang a number of times before he hung up. She was not there. A moment later, as he was wondering what to do next, the instrument jangled beside him.

"Hello."

"Frank? This is Fogherty. Look, I remembered I had an old uniform that's too small for me. I called Sandy and she dug it out, says it's in good shape, and she's going to pack it up and mail it. Should be here in the morning."

"Fine," Frank said. "Listen, Jim, where are you?"

Fogherty was in his room.

"Well, can you meet me downstairs in the bar in about ten minutes? I want to fill you in on a few more details."

"Okay, fine by me. See you there."

Frank hung up. Then he got out a pencil and piece of paper and wrote a note.

*Vikki*, it read, *I am leaving tonight for home—if you want a lift part of the way, meet me behind the restaurant about ten. Will try to have Fogherty's car there and we'll drive into the city. If you can't get free, try to let me know in advance.*
                                                                    *Frank*

He gathered up the rest of his papers quickly and shredded them into the washbasin. Then he fired a match and touched it to the mass of confetti. It burned down to a powdery ash which he washed down the drain, leaving only faint yellow marks where the heat had scorched the porcelain. "Add it on my bill," he muttered, going to the bedroom again. He finished packing and stacked his suitcase by the head of the bed. Going out, he twisted the key in the lock to his room, then turned around.

"Hello, genius."

Jay Ginther sat loose-sprawled on the couch in the center of the room. As Frank frowned at him, the young man got slowly to his feet and walked a few leisurely steps forward, then stopped. "Hope you don't mind a friendly little visit?"

"Make yourself at home," Frank said, ignoring the thinly concealed sneer on the other's face.

"Well, thanks... thanks a lot. You're a real neighborly guy, aren't you?" The smile faded quickly, like a tropical sunset, leaving dark clouds of hatred in his eyes. "Too neighborly, maybe."

"Something on your mind, Ginther?" He wondered if this was Hanford's answer to him, coming already.

"Yeah, something's on my mind. I'm wondering what to do about a guy that comes muscling in where he doesn't belong, taking everything over."

Frank understood men. He grinned. This had nothing to do with his argument with Hanford. "Got you worried, huh?" he said.

"Sure. So worried I can't sleep at night," the other man said evenly. "I just wander around, thinking about my troubles—and keeping my eyes open for things that happen real late-like."

Frank tensed, the memory of the half-seen figure in the darkness the previous evening clearly etched in his brain. Ginther stared back at him, something alive and ugly stirring deep in his eyes.

"So what can I do about it?" Frank asked.

"That's what I was wondering," Ginther said slowly. "Then, last night, it all of the sudden came to me. Last night I figured out what it was you could do."

"What?"

For the first time, the blond-haired man smiled.

"Die," he said quietly, then turned and walked away.

Frank fought back an urge to go after Ginther, holding himself against the rising pressure of rage. He realized he was gripping the edge of the bar counter, and as his fingers started aching he released his hold, turning away in disgust. Smashing the cocky gunman's face in would be a luxury—one he couldn't afford if his planned escape was to succeed. Forget Ginther—the younger man was no threat at the moment anyway. He wouldn't dare to interfere with Frank before Hanford's job had been accomplished.

He glanced at his watch, saw it was time to meet Fogherty and went downstairs to the bar. The big man was sitting in one of the vacant booths near the door, taking swallows from a large double-shotglass.

"Hello, Shelby," he said as Frank slid in across from him. A waiter came over and Frank ordered coffee. "Another of these for me," Fogherty said.

"Nothing more for you," Frank said evenly.

Fogherty stared. "What?"

"I said nothing more for you." He looked up at the waiter. "That's all," he said and waited until the man walked away.

"Hey, what do you—"

"Shut up," Frank said. "Keep your mouth shut and listen if you want to go on living for a while."

Fogherty gaped at him, stunned.

"Now answer my questions and answer them straight, mister. First of all, you've never worked on a heist before, is that right?" Frank nodded. "That's what I thought. But you got in a little deep in the dice room here, and you suddenly decided you could be a bank robber—to square your debt with Hanford."

Fogherty was looking down at his glass, his hands shaking.

"Did you tell him you'd worked on jobs before? Whose name did you use to put you in on a deal like this."

The big man shook his head. "I didn't—"

"No? And Hanford never asked you? Just said, 'Okay, come on along, we'll stick up a bank together'? Think that over, Fogherty—think what it means that a professional crook doesn't even ask you if you know what you're doing when you come to him with a fancy idea for a job."

"I tipped him," Fogherty said, his voice near a whine. "I'm giving all the information. That's why he cut me in."

"And just what good are you after you've given all your information," Frank asked.

"Why, I—"

"You're no good at all—that's the answer to that one, Fogherty." He leaned forward. "That's why Hanford has decided to get rid of you—he told me this afternoon."

The terror that had started to kindle in the big man's eyes flamed high. His voice rose. "I don't believe you," he cried. "You're lying!"

"*Shut up, you fat son of a bitch!*" Frank hissed. He looked around quickly. The waiter came over with the cup of coffee and set it down. Frank tipped him, and he left.

Fogherty's face was sallow. "I don't believe you," he repeated.

Frank stared at him, expressionless.

"Why—why would he?" Fogherty stammered. "I don't understand."

"Number one, because you welshed on a debt; number two, because you're an outsider who knows too much about the gang now. Hanford probably doesn't have any choice, you know; if he didn't want to kill you the others would force him to do it—or do it themselves."

The ashen skin of Fogherty's face was suddenly loose and sunken looking. He understood now why the others had not been very friendly with him from the beginning. He understood—and knew that what Frank said was true.

"What can I do?" he mumbled.

"That's better. Now listen—we're getting out of here tonight—you, me and Vikki. We're clearing out late, about ten o'clock, when they think we've all settled down." Frank leaned closer, lowering his voice.

Fogherty looked at him with sudden hope. "You think we can?"

"With luck it'll be easy. They figure I have no means of travel, and they don't suspect you know anything. Say you're going to talk to your friend at the O'Farrell Company—say you can get some more dope on the transfer. Then drive back this evening, park out back. We'll meet you about ten."

"What'll he do when he finds out?"

"Hanford? There's not much he can do. We'll all have gone in different directions, and if we're in it together he won't dare go for one of us without first finding the rest."

"Why are you doing this for me?"

"I'm not," Frank said harshly. "I wouldn't walk across the street to save your hind end, Fogherty. I figure you got yourself into this, you should pay the price."

"Then—"

"For one thing, you're helping me out by doing it this way. I need you. For another, say that I feel sorry for your wife Sandy. I'd like to see her get a break, I'd like to see you go back and straighten things out with her and give her the kind of life she deserves."

The big man seemed on the verge of breaking down. He nodded, controlling himself, and said, "All right. I'll do it—I'll be there."

"Good," Frank said, standing up. "Don't mess it up." He turned to go.

"Shelby?" the man at the table said.

Frank stopped. "Yes?"

"Thanks—thanks for both of us, Sandy and me."

"Forget it." He tapped Fogherty on the shoulder and went out of the bar, back up to his room.

He checked his watch—it was after two-thirty. He decided he wasn't hungry and that he could eat before it was time to go. There was no message from Vikki as yet, and her phone still did not answer when he tried it again. He stretched out on the couch and prepared to wait.

# CHAPTER SEVEN

I T WAS A LITTLE before nine o'clock in the evening. Frank Shelby sat up and slipped his stockinged feet into his shoes, then went into the bathroom and tossed cold water over his face. The pent-up exhaustion in his body had brought brief snatches of sleep in the hours just past—not enough to help, just enough to leave him with a turning feeling in his stomach.

He put on a tie, knotted it with quick twists of his hands, then went across to the telephone. "Hello, this is Shelby. I'd like some dinner—a steak, medium-rare, and..." He paused to make his change of mind convincing, then said, "No, wait a minute. On second thought, I believe I'll eat in the dining room. Never mind." He hung up. Unless he guessed wrong, Hanford would know everything he did; this should help further the impression that he was not planning anything this night. The old man might even think he had changed his mind. He finished dressing and left the room.

The lights in the living room were not on, and Frank didn't bother to use them. In the deep quiet of the room he moved across to the door leading to Hanford's apartments and listened. There was no sound. He paused, looking down at the dimly lit interior of the aquarium, seeing the slowly stirring red bodies settling for the night.

Wonder what he feeds you? Frank thought. He flicked a finger into the water, watching the ripples spread. The fish below took no notice. If I guess wrong tonight, it's fresh food for the next few days, friends. With a wry grin, he turned away and crossed the room. He stepped outside and closed the door.

The hall was empty, noises drifting up from below. He descended the stairs, noticing that the club seemed well filled and very busy. Crowds of laughing, prosperous people pushed through the lobby, parting reluctantly for Frank as he made his way toward the dining room. He tried to see if he was being watched, but the press of the crowd around him was too great, and he gave up looking. At the entrance to the main dining room the maître d' nodded and stepped forward.

"By yourself, sir?"

"Yes," Frank said.

"This way." Frank followed the tuxedoed little man down to the front of the big room, near the stage that resembled an open clearing under the skies, where he had seen Vikki again that first night—how long ago? Up close, he could see that the pool was larger than he'd first thought, extending back between the rocks and out of sight to the rear. Lights just below the surface, beaming downward, indicated a considerable depth, and a persistent humming sound marked the steady inward flow of filtered water.

He ordered lavishly—filet mignon on the full dinner. When his food came, however, he concentrated on the thick cut of steak, slicing the tender reddish meat into thin, medallion-sized strips, and chewing them down. He glanced at his watch regularly. Vikki's first show had ended just before he came in, and another was not due till eleven. They would have ample time to reach town before her absence was discovered. As the minute hand of his watch neared the top of the dial, Frank looked up and signaled his waitress.

He asked the girl a question and listened to her answer. He thanked her, put his napkin on his chair and moved across the room to the near wall. Once there, however, he did not turn in the direction the girl had given him but went quickly to his right instead, through the door to the kitchen.

He walked into a scene of purposeful activity. Cooks in white uniforms hurried about their jobs, tending the huge stoves and refrigerators. A dish-washing machine ground away at its task with an angry clatter in one corner of the large room. Waitresses, less romantic in the bright light but no less handsome in their gauzy uniforms, rushed back and forth through the set of palm-camouflaged doors leading to the dining room. No one paid him any attention as he went on through the kitchen and out its back door.

It was cool and dark in the alley, the noises of the busy restaurant only dimly heard from within. The brick wall of a large storehouse faced him from across the narrow driveway, either end opening out onto the parking lot. In the moment it took for his eyes to adjust to the lack of light, Frank strained his ears for a sound—then heard the quiet, steady thrum of an idling engine. It was to his left.

He quit the shadow of the doorway, moving cautiously down the paved strip, clinging close to the side of the building. At the end of the alley he stopped and looked out. Fogherty's car was parked close to the wall of the storehouse, out of the reflected glare of the parking lot lights farther up front. Its engine was running, a trickle of white smoke rising in the air from its exhaust. He stepped away from the protection of the building and sprinted to the car. He grabbed the door and started to open it, then stopped. The seats were empty.

The discovery jolted him. Fogherty and Vikki should have been here, ready to go. He didn't understand—where could they have gone? Were they somewhere nearby, waiting for him, or had they been here and for some reason had to leave? Still confused, he pulled open the door and took another look. Still nothing.

Then he heard it.

It was a scuffling, grating sound, directly behind him. Instinctively, he whirled, crouched. But he was too late. The pair of figures bore in like evil shadows—a large man and a smaller one. In the pale glow from the floodlights in front of the Xanadu, Frank saw the outline of a man's face—the smaller of the two—and saw the brief gleam of gold hair. Then a solid arc of blackness swept toward him. He felt the popping burst of pain against his head, the silent roar and motionless fall, until all the world about became a formless, softening thing—and was no more.

He knew—had known for some time—that he was on the floor of an automobile in the back seat. He wondered if he were tied very tightly, left lying face down and helpless, or if he could move at all. But it was some time before he decided to try. The car was not running, so perhaps there was no one around. His left hand lifted quite easily, touching his throbbing head, but he couldn't seem to budge the other. Then he realized this was because he was lying on it. He heaved his body upward, but collapsed as a wave of pain struck with the force of remembered blows. His arm was free now, though. Soon it began to tingle with needle-jabs of returning circulation; the prickly sensation was almost welcome—it helped clear his mind.

Slowly, he remembered where he was.

Fogherty's car. He had been about to get in it. Who had hit him? Oh yes, that lousy stench, that scrubby two-bit dirt-eating bastard. But where were they now? Carefully, he worked both arms to a position of leverage against the floor and tried to raise himself. Halfway up, the hammers began on his head again, and he groaned involuntarily and froze. Still no sound. He decided there was definitely no one in the car. Less cautiously, he pushed himself on up. He was wrong. There was someone else in the car, the top of his head just showing above the back of the front seat. It was Fogherty.

And he was very dead.

He looked out of the car and saw nothing but a line of houses facing him on the near side of the street. Across from where they were parked, however, and down about a half a block, were the lights of a coffee shop, blinking on and off. The sign in front said,

WE NEVER CLOSE. He rubbed his head gingerly, wincing at the pain, and located a sticky area behind his right ear, the wetness running down his neck and into his collar. His scalp was cut, but not badly, and the bleeding seemed to have stopped. The rest of his face felt puffed and swollen, and he gradually became aware of the particular areas of soreness—his lips, which felt thick and puffed on one side, his temple and cheekbone, where the lower lid of his eye was swollen almost shut. His chest and ribs were the worst—they ached painfully with each breath he took. He explored for broken ribs, but each touch sent fingers of pain through him, and he gave up.

It occurred to him, then, that he was sitting alone—at night—with a murdered man in the car. They had left him here. What if he hadn't come to before he was discovered? Of course, though, that was the idea—that was how it was supposed to happen. He had to get out of here, he had to get away.

Wait. Maybe the car would still run … no, not smart. They probably had a stolen report on it already.

Christ! he told himself. Stop stalling—you can figure it out later. Get moving.

He shoved open the back door and climbed achingly out of the car. Looking in at the slumped form, he felt sudden pity and guilt, as though he should have done something more—got Fogherty out of range before they'd had a chance to do this to him. After all, if the big man hadn't come back for him with the car …

No—that was wrong. Fogherty had been doomed from the start. If anything, Frank had brought hope where there was none—for a little while, anyway.

Must try to explain that to Sandy, he thought bitterly.

There was no use wasting time, now. One of the gang might be around the neighborhood to see what developed. He began walking toward the lights of the café he'd seen up ahead. There would be a telephone there. He could call a cab. Halfway to the place, he stopped. It was a trap. They had deliberately parked him in sight of the café. They had wanted him to walk into the brightly lighted room so that he could be identified later. He felt a shudder of nervousness at how close he'd come to falling for it.

Lights flashed behind him. He turned and saw a car swinging onto the street, several blocks away. Going into a crouch, he sprinted for a low hedge in front of the row of houses and dropped behind it, shafts of pain exploding through his body. He lay still, teeth clenched in agony as the current of hurt subsided. Then he raised his head enough to see through the foliage.

It was a police car.

Breath choking inside him, he watched hypnotically as the car cruised along the quiet street. Suddenly its search beam flicked on and swept the side of Fogherty's car. The cruiser seemed to slow, then picked up again and went on past, giving a single, sharp blast of its horn. It continued up the street, pulling into the parking lot of the diner.

Frank let out the lungful of air he'd been holding with a hiss of relief. Apparently they'd thought the figure slumped in the front seat was asleep. He stood up and stepped back onto the sidewalk. He didn't have long—and he was on foot. Somehow, he must get out of the neighborhood before the body was found and a search begun. There was a filling station some distance up the road in the direction of the all night restaurant, and he decided to make for it.

*Wait.*

A danger signal seemed to go off in his brain—something he had forgot. Panic fingered his throat, but he drove it back with an angry shrug. Carefully, methodically, he sent his mind exploring for the flaw in the last few moments—he had awakened in the car, Fogherty dead in front, the plant set up to pin the murder on him …

Then he knew.

The car would have been rigged—fingerprints probably and, most certainly of all, a weapon.

He had to go back to the car. Turning, he walked as quickly as he was able toward the ominous shape. Any minute, he knew, the policemen would come out of the diner and see that the car had not moved. They would come back to take more direct methods for waking the driver. He broke into a ragged trot, each footfall sending a sword of pain up into his body.

When he reached the car he circled around to the curb-side and pulled open the front and back doors, using his handkerchief on each of the metal parts. Now he had to find the weapon. The wound in Fogherty's head told him he was looking for a gun.

It was not on the floor in the back seat as he had supposed it would be. He felt down the cushions and found nothing. In front, then! Quickly he made a check of the floor and seat up front—then frisked the dead man lightly. Still nothing. Fear returned, insistently this time, brushing aside his calm and his logic, forcing a small cry of anger and despair from his swollen lips. It had to be under the seat—but he couldn't see. A match! He fumbled in his coat, found a nearly empty book and pulled two of the matches in it loose in his fingers. He struck at the package clumsily, dropped them, tore out another. This he struck and stooped to see with. It flickered out in his grasp. Another, quickly! The packet was empty.

Almost crying with rage, he tried to jam his hand beneath the seat, but there was not room. He was about to give up and flee heedlessly when he thought of a flashlight. Running around the car, he pulled open the right-front door and jerked at the glove compartment. With frozen horror, he saw up ahead the shafting beam of the restaurant door opening, the pair of uniformed figures stepping out. They paused, looking toward the car. Crouched behind the half-open door, Frank wondered if they'd seen him. Mechanically, his hands kept working at the compartment; it fell open. There was no flashlight inside—then his clawing hand fell on cold metal.

The gun.

He stuffed it in his pocket and slid down flat to the pavement, letting the door close above him. Scrabbling backwards, he worked around to the rear of the car, keeping it between himself and the line of vision of the patrol vehicle. He waited while the headlights flashed past him in a flat arc as the police car swung out into the street and headed his way. Then he drove his legs, pistoning across the sidewalk, up onto the lawn and into the protective shadow of the house.

Praying there would be no dog, he ran on, no longer feeling the jabbing protest of his muscles, swinging over the fence at the rear of the house and into a densely grown vacant lot. He kept going across the lot and out onto the street behind. The filling station he had seen would be up ahead. It was a risk, but he'd have to take it. As he half-walked, half-trotted, he tried to keep watch through the houses to the street behind. Once he thought he saw a light slant between the row of houses—the patrol car, beginning its first, hurried search—but it was moving in the opposite direction.

The filling station faced the street where Fogherty's car was parked, so that Frank approached it now from the rear, staying out of the circle of lights in front. He slipped across the paved lot to the washroom, closing the door softly as he went in, then locking it. Outside, he heard the even strokes of a broom—the attendant sweeping away a coating of water and gasoline, cleaning the aprons for the night. He sighed deeply, resting his face against the cool, white wall. For the moment he was safe.

He had to clean himself first. His puffed and discolored face looked back at him discouragingly in the mirror. It was going to look bad anyway, but he would do what he could. He stripped off his coat and shirt, laying them across the waste-paper receptacle while the basin filled with water. Disgustedly, he found there was no hot tap—he would have to use cold. First he washed his face carefully, then laved water over the top of his head with his hands. It colored the bowl a dull brown from the loose blood on his scalp, and he changed the water twice before the discoloration stopped. He blotted his hair dry with paper towels. Pressure on the tender area at the back of his skull still revealed a dull stain on the paper, but there was only a slow ooze from the wound. He combed all of his head but the cut part, smoothing the hair over it with his hands.

The swelling on his face did not seem to respond to the cold wash, but part of the redness and the violent, angry look of the dried blood was gone. He definitely needed an ice pack for the eye and side of his mouth, but there was no helping that.

Next, his clothes. His coat was dusty and smudged, but the only real damage seemed to be a tear at one elbow. He dusted the coat and damped the deeper stains with a wet towel. His shirt collar had blood on it, but not as much as he'd feared—only a small splotch where one thin trickle had run down his neck. Washing it, he knew, would do no good. He patted cold water onto his chest and ribs to relieve the smarting, then reversed the white shirt and put it back on. This required buttoning it upside-down—pushing the small pearl disks down through the holes where they touched his hot skin and folding the collar backwards; with his coat on it would stay down. The stain had not come through, and with his tie in place to hide the inverted buttons he could get by. With a final look in the mirror, Frank switched out the light and went to the door.

There were no unusual sounds from outside. He opened a slit through which to scout the View and saw the lot was still empty. He slipped outside, moving across to one corner of the parking area where a telephone booth was standing. He stepped in and closed the door, noting from the corner of his eye that the station attendant had looked over and had seen him. For a moment he was poised to run again, but then the attendant went back to his sweeping. Apparently he didn't know what had happened yet. The cop car hadn't been here. Swiftly, Frank dialed the number of a cab company.

He gave the address of a house he had passed a few minutes before on the way to the filling station—one in front of which a porch-light had been burning. The call completed, he stepped out of the booth, turned and started down the street away from the direction of the number he'd given. He didn't turn to look, but he hoped that the station attendant would remark his passing. At the corner Frank cut across the street and stopped, out of the beam of the streetlight. When he was certain no one observed, he began to make his way back again. Clinging close to the shadows on the far side of the pavement, he reached the place again quickly. The slow minutes began to tick by. Just as he decided the cab was definitely not coming, lights turned onto the street. He stepped back alongside the house, watching the approaching car. It stopped at the foot of the walk and sounded its horn. It was the taxi.

Frank stepped out briskly, as though coming from the rear, and went down to the waiting car. He ducked his head to the cabbie and slid into the rear seat, keeping his face hidden by the shadows.

"Idlewild," he said, "and make it fast."

"Right," said the driver. They pulled away into the darkness. He watched out the rear for several minutes, then finally relaxed. They had not been followed.

There had been only one cancellation on the 5:30 A.M. flight to Blaine. He was fifth in line for it on the gate list, but when boarding started he went in through the line with the confirmed passengers and took a seat near the front of the plane. There had been a moment's confusion when the stewardess thought she had room for another replacement, but when she found Frank already in his seat she apparently thought he had been sent ahead by the purser. After long minutes of agony, expecting a running figure to come out from the terminal gate any minute, Frank saw the cabin door close and heard the engines begin to turn, one by one. He was lucky—he didn't think he could have lasted the wait for another plane.

He slept most of the trip, waking at last only when the increasing air-pressure on his eardrums told him they were descending again. In a few minutes, he thought, I will see her, and I'll hold her a long, long time before I tell her anything. Somehow, I'll make her understand. Perhaps, he thought, they could run away, find something to sustain them through yet another beginning—be more careful this time. He hoped so. ... No, he was sure of it.

He had no trouble finding a cab and gave the driver his address. Then he sat tensely, watching out the window, pleading inside himself for the car to hurry and get him home. Never had he longed so desperately for Nancy.

They turned, at last, onto his street, and the taxi pulled slowly to the curb. There were no other cars around, so perhaps word had not reached her yet. With luck, she might still be in bed, unaware of his return, or of its implications.

He still had quite a bit of money left. They had not taken that when they'd beaten him. He paid the cabbie with part of it and went to the front door.

He had his key out, but then decided not to risk frightening his wife. He rang. Seconds passed and there was no sound from within. He rang again, more insistently this time, and again waited. At last, unreasoning fear starting up within in, he inserted the key in the lock and went in. The house was quiet, empty.

Puzzled, he closed the door. Quietly, moving with instinctive if not too logical caution, he went to their bedroom. No one was there. She had not left unexpectedly—the bed was made, no clothes were lying about. The rest of the rooms were similarly neat and mute. At last he went into the kitchen, confusion gripping his tired mind. Could she be at her father's? There was no reason to suppose so, yet it seemed the only possible solution. Certainly there had not been time since he'd left New York for her to receive any kind of word about him. Or, if she had, to have left everything so well arranged.

Still wondering over the matter, he began putting on a pan of water to heat for some instant coffee—then he saw the telegram.

He sat down suddenly at the table, his hands falling on the white formica top before him. Slowly, automatically, he picked it up and began to read:

DARLING—HAVE COMPLETED WONDERFUL DEAL WITH HANFORD FIRM HERE IN NEW YORK—WILL BE STAYING ON—CAN MAKE ALL ARRANGEMENTS THERE LATER— WOULD LIKE YOU TO JOIN ME NOW—NEED YOUR OPINION— URGENT YOU HURRY—TICKETS ON NEXT PLANE TO NEW YORK RESERVED—HANFORD'S CHAUFFEUR WILL MEET YOU.

LOVE—FRANK

"They've got her," he mumbled in disbelief. "They've got Nancy...."

# CHAPTER EIGHT

THE PLANE TRIP BACK to New York had not been difficult to arrange. He had got a reservation on the first flight out and had been left with just enough time to make a trip downtown, purchase a shoulder harness and cartridges for the gun he had taken from Fogherty's car, draw out the balance of his bank savings and return to the airport. It was still early morning.

The trip seemed endless. And when, at last, they did arrive, he had difficulty finding a taxi right away. It was almost noon when he finally pulled up in front of *Club Xanadu*. The parking lot was nearly deserted.

Frank paid the cab-driver, tipped him heavily rather than wait for change and ran quickly up the stairs into the building. There were a few people in at the bar, but the lobby was deserted except for the Arab-looking doorman in white burnoose and turban whom he'd seen before. He nodded and turned to go up the stairs, a sense of urgency filling him now. At the top of the steps he heard a noise and stopped. He looked back and saw the white-clad man behind him. He reached for the lapel of his coat, but at that instant the other man produced a hand from under his robes—as though by a trick of conjure, the hand contained a revolver.

"I wouldn't do that," a voice said, and the voice was Jay Ginther's.

Frank stared.

Ginther laughed, slipping off the turban. "We've been expecting you," he said. "Cat was at the airport to meet you, but apparently you didn't see him. He took the trouble to phone ahead. Anything we can do for you?"

Frank cursed himself for a fool. He had blundered in like a drunk husband at a ladies' social, and now he was trapped. "I want to talk to Hanford," he muttered.

"Sure. Easy done. Turn around first and lean against that wall with both hands."

Carefully, he turned around and walked to the wall. From the corner of his eye he watched Ginther, saw that the man was following him closely. Too closely. He gauged his distance carefully and stopped.

"Lean," Ginther repeated.

Frank shifted his weight forward, but his hands missed the wall by inches, and he bent at the waist swiftly, reaching back to clamp his hands around the blond man's ankle. A blast sounded over his head, a bullet slammed into the wall just as he jerked. Ginther fell hard on his back, the wind going out of him in an explosive grunt. Frank brought his heel down hard on the hand with the gun, then toed it away from the broken fingers. He pulled Jay to his feet and forced him back against the wall.

"Now, you son of a bitch, let's see if you remember—"

He hit carefully, to avoid hurting his hands. He hooked into the body from the right, then the left, hitting along the ribs and in the stomach, not hitting the heart because that would bring on unconsciousness. Ginther made deep, animal sounds of pain, jolting back to the wall after each blow, trying to double down away from the thudding fists but pinned by Frank's weight. When the noises no longer followed each blow, Shelby shifted his attention to the distorted face.

He chopped a left, aiming for the cheek, but he hit a little short. His blow fell on the mouth, and he felt the flesh tear on his knuckles. Ginther opened his lips as though smiling. Two teeth fell out and he looked down at them, blood spurting over the front of his white robes. Frank hit him with his right, more accurately this time. The cheek split open below Ginther's left eye. The gunman's head snapped back under the impact, then came forward off the wall. Frank said, "God damn you," and hit straight into the exposed face. He felt bone and cartilage give, spreading under his fist, heard the strangled cry Ginther uttered, and let the senseless man crash to the floor. Frank stood, breathing in desperate gasps, his lungs and throat burning from the unusual exertion. His own body throbbed as painfully from the exertion as if he'd received the same blows Ginther had.

"Nicely done," Arnie Benson said from behind him.

Frank whirled around. Hines was there too, looking down at the figure crumpled on the floor. "But if you try it on me," Arnie continued, "I'll have to put one through you. Now pass over the heat—quick!"

Shelby stared at the big man a moment and knew his fight was over. The automatic enveloped in Benson's huge hand was unwavering. Slowly, he unfastened his shoulder holster and let it drop to the carpet.

"Now, let's go down the hall," Benson said. "Joe, take care of Jay here." He motioned to Frank with his gun, and they started walking.

Hanford was waiting in the living room, seated in a straight-backed chair and staring morosely out at the sun-deck. He turned as they came in and nodded to Frank, indicating the couch with one hand. "Sit down, Frank," he said. "You made a fast trip, I see."

Benson signaled to Hanford. "Our boy's feeling a little nasty. Better watch him—he just roughed Jay up pretty bad."

The old man looked curiously at Frank, then back to Arnie. "I see," he said. "But I'm sure Frank thinks too much of his wife to cause me any trouble at this time. Don't you, Frank?"

"Where is she?" Shelby demanded through clenched teeth.

"Now, now, my boy, you know I wouldn't let anything happen to Nancy."

*"Where is she, I asked you!"* He came forward on his seat tensely, as though ready to spring for the old man's throat.

Hanford glanced calmly past him to where Benson was standing, then met Frank's eyes again—a warning against any try at violence. "She's here, of course," he said, "and quite safe. You may see her, but only after we have come to a little better agreement than we have apparently had in the past."

Frank stared at him, containing his hatred.

"You are not going to cause me any more trouble, Frank— you may as well know that. You should have known, of course, that I had no intention of letting you walk out on me at such a crucial time. The beating you were given was by way of a warning—unpleasant for me but quite necessary, I thought."

"Sorry it upset you."

Hanford acknowledged this with a nod. "Jay acted quite without orders in the matter of leaving you with the body, I'm afraid," he added. "Fortunately, nothing resulted from it, and I reprimanded him."

Frank thought, So did I, but held his silence.

"The main thing," Hanford went on, "is for you to understand how foolish any repetition would be. Your wife will remain here under constant guard. If you do not complete your bargain with me, both you and she will suffer for it. I suppose that's clear?"

Frank nodded, a knot of defeat slowly forming in his chest. He was conscious again of the stabbing pains and the physical weakness he felt. He'd had his chance—and failed. Hanford was not the kind to be caught off guard again. His next words confirmed it.

"In fact, I must tell you that you too will be carefully watched from now on till the completion of the crime. I had given you freedom of movement, but now that must unfortunately cease. You will stay in these apartments at all times, unless accompanied by someone else."

"For another whole week?"

Hanford frowned. "That is another thing," he said. Frank saw with surprise that there was worry and a quick look of strain in the old man's face. "The day of transfer has been unexpectedly changed, I fear," he said.

"What? Why?"

"I don't know. It happened just after your last conversation with Mr. Fogherty. He panicked, of course, and came to me in a near hysterical state."

That explained why his escape plan had backfired.

"I suppose Jim had rather good reason to be nervous," Hanford added dubiously. "One can't help wondering if the change of date suggests a possible knowledge on the bank's part that something is planned." The lines of worry deepened across the small man's forehead. "If so, I imagine we can thank him for that, too. In any case, we are going ahead."

Hanford reached over to the table beside him and picked up a calf-bound notebook lying there. He handed the book to Frank. "These are Jim's notes—the rest of the information on the transfer you may not have. Look it over and check it with your plans. See that everything is all right, and we will schedule a meeting for later this afternoon so that you can give final instructions."

A suspicion tugged at the corner of his mind. "Final instructions?" he said. "When is the new date?"

The old man hesitated. "Tomorrow night," he said then.

*"Tomorrow!"*

Hanford looked up quickly, his mouth set in a grim line. "The trucks have been prepared as you instructed. The other materials—maps, guard uniform and such—have been placed in your room. Unless you have withheld something, we are ready."

"But it's impossible. The men haven't had time to go through their jobs, check the timing, look over the route or anything else!"

"Then your instructions will have to be very complete and explicit."

Frank's mouth opened, but words did not come.

"For I hardly need tell you, a great deal depends upon the success of this robbery. For you, personally, and for your wife." Hanford stood up.

"And now, if you're ready, I will ask that charming lady to come in. I'm sure you're anxious to see her." He nodded at Benson, and the big man moved over to the telephone. Hanford turned back to Frank. "I needn't warn you about the dangers of alarming her. I have had the men follow the plan of telling her you are working on a contracting job. You will be careful, I hope?"

A few minutes later, the front door opened. Nancy came in with Cat behind her. Hanford went forward quickly to meet them.

"Ah, Mrs. Shelby! I am Stanley Hanford, so pleased to meet you at last. And here is the husband I have been so thoughtlessly keeping from you!"

Nancy smiled a little, ill at ease, then glanced at Frank. Her eyes widened when she saw his marked face, and she ran to him. He caught her in his arms. "Oh, darling," she whispered. "Oh, darling what happened?"

"Nothing, Nan, I'm all right." He moved her gently back from him, turning her toward the small man again.

As though he had seen nothing unusual in any of this, Hanford said, "You know Cat, of course, and I think you've met most of my other associates. In any case, you'll see everyone later, at dinner or tomorrow during the day. But now I imagine you'd like to be alone with your husband for a while before seeing your room?"

Nancy looked back coldly. "I'll be staying here, then?"

The little man seemed surprised. "Why, I supposed that you would want to, yes." He spread his small hands expressively. "Did you have other plans?"

"No, I was only wondering," she said. "Suppose, though, I wanted to go to a hotel?"

"But, my dear girl," the old man said, the cordial smile on his face tightening slightly. "If it is not the question, why do you ask?"

Frank heard his wife's voice grow stronger, as she ignored the question to ask one of her own. It was as though she were trying to show him something—perhaps to make Hanford reveal his true motives in case Frank did not see them.

"Suppose I wanted to go into the city tomorrow to do some shopping?"

Mr. Hanford's lips barely turned upwards at their corners. "Of course, it is just a matter of a day or two until you both will be returning to the city. I can't imagine that you would want anything we do not have here for at least that long."

There was a short silence, then Nancy said, "I see." She turned to Frank, her eyes hopelessly questioning.

"And now then, if you folks will just make yourselves at home, I'll leave you for a while. If there's anything you lack, just phone for it." Hanford moved toward the front door. "It's been a pleasure meeting you, Mrs. Shelby. I'll look forward to talking with you again soon. For now, good night." The door closed behind the small, black-clad figure.

Nancy threw herself into Frank's arms, her body shaking with sobs. "Oh, darling," she cried, "oh, Frank, what is it? What's wrong with everyone here?" Her shoulders jerked convulsively, her words choked off by the sobs. He pressed her to him tightly, stroking the taut curve of her back and speaking softly.

"It's all right, Nan. Please believe me, it's going to be all right."

After a few moments she began to regain control of herself, and the sobs slowly died. He led her to the couch, and they sat down together. When she turned to him, her face was lowered so that he would not see the streaking tears there. "I'm sorry, darling, I didn't mean to act like a baby. Frank, what's wrong? I want you to tell me. Who are these men—what are you doing here?"

"Nan—"

"It's something bad, isn't it, Frank?" she rushed on. "It isn't what you told me it would be, what that man pretends. It isn't construction work, is it?"

Slowly, he shook his head. "No, it's not."

"Then what, Frank, *what?*"

"Nan, I—I don't know how to say this to you. I don't want you to misunderstand. But I can't answer any of your questions."

Her face was puzzled. "You can't answer?"

He nodded. "That's right. I would like to tell you but you'll have to trust me, darling. For a while, at least."

She looked at him in disbelief. "I—I don't understand, Frank."

He struggled for something to say, some explanation that could possibly satisfy her. There was none. There was only the truth, and for the sake of what small chance of survival she might have, he dared not tell that.

"It's very important that you pretend to believe everything they tell you," he explained in a soft tone. "No matter what you think, or what you feel, you must act as though everything were perfectly all right and just the way you expected it. Can you do that?"

Her amazement seemed to grow and deepen. She sat back in the cushions, still looking at him. "Well, in that case … " she said, her voice trailing off. He saw that she was hurt and unhappy. He wanted to say more, but no words came to his lips.

"I think," Nancy said deliberately, "that I would like a drink."

"Sure, I'll get it." He jumped up and went to the bar. "Martini all right?" She nodded. As he fixed the drink he watched her across the room. She got up and walked over to the huge aquarium. She stood looking down into the tank.

"What strange fish," she said.

"Yes, they are, aren't they? One of Hanford's hobbies."

She came over to the bar and took her glass. Her eyes were steady now, and clear. She clicked her glass against his and sipped at the whitish-green liquid. When she put the glass down she was even smiling a little. "All right, then," she said quietly. "If you think best."

He took her hands in his and pulled her forward. They kissed across the bar-top, and then he looked hard into her face and felt a sudden, leaden sadness. With one hand he touched the line of her jaw, tracing it down to the petite, pointed chin. "You're very wonderful, Nan," he said softly. "I wish you could know how much I love you, darling."

She smiled and leaned forward again, their lips about to touch—when there was a sharp rapping at the door. With an expression of annoyance, Frank went around the end of the bar and across to the entrance. Hines was standing in the hall.

"I'll show Mrs. Shelby to her room now," he said.

"She's not quite ready," Frank told him.

The slender man did not move, his face impassive. "Mr. Hanford says you have some things to work on before the meeting. Now would be a good time for Mrs. Shelby to get settled."

For an instant anger flared in him, but Nancy was standing at his side and touched his arm lightly.

"I'll go now, darling. We can see each other later."

He looked down, and her eyes asked him not to lose his temper.

"All right," he said, not looking at Hines. Though it was just mid-afternoon, a quick stock of his rapidly ebbing strength told him he couldn't go on much longer. After the meeting he would be finished, he knew.

"I don't know about dinner tonight," he said. "The way I feel—"

Nancy understood. "Never mind, darling," she said gently. "I'll be all right. You rest, and I'll see you in the morning."

He looked down at her gratefully. "You call if everything isn't all right."

"I will," she promised.

Nancy stood on tiptoes and kissed him lightly. Then she went out into the hall. He closed the door and walked back into the living room. The notebook was on the table where Hanford had left it. Slowly, he went over and picked it up, began leafing through the pages. After a moment, he lowered his throbbing body to the couch again and started studying Fogherty's notes with great intensity.

An hour later, when the others arrived for the meeting, they found Frank Shelby surrounded by papers—Fogherty's writings and the maps that had been procured at Frank's request. The latter he was busily marking with pen and ink.

"Can we interrupt you now?" Hanford asked, coming in. He was followed by Benson, Cat and Hines. Ginther was not with them.

"Yes, just finishing," Frank said, looking up at them all.

The others took seats about the room, silent and disturbed, it seemed. There was a tension among them that reflected their nervousness at the sudden alteration in plans.

"Where's Ginther?" Frank asked with a slightly malicious smile. The men seemed unwilling to meet his gaze.

"Jay will receive his instructions through me," Hanford said, frowning. "I think it better the two of you remain apart until after this is over."

Frank nodded. "Fine," he said.

"Shall we begin, then?"

Frank had committed his work to memory, then burned his notes in the sink. Knowledge was his only life insurance, and the more of it he had the safer he and Nancy were. For a few hours, at any rate.

Frank saw the others looking at him expectantly. "I've marked these maps with the course each of us will follow tomorrow night," he said. "On these pieces of paper I've put down each man's job and made up timetables that show where to be—and when." He handed the papers around, giving Ginther's to the old man.

"What are our chances?" Joe Hines asked suddenly.

Frank was taken partially by surprise. He looked around and saw that the others in the room approved of the slender man's question; the possibility of failure—which had seemed so mysteriously absent in them at the beginning—was now present. Only Hanford seemed unaware of it. He glanced up and said, "The same as they were before, wouldn't you say, Frank?"

Shelby nodded. "About the same," he said. And I'd hate to tell you what that is, he thought. You wouldn't like it much.

"Let's go over it once," Frank said. "Arnie?"

The big man looked up.

"You're going to drive the tow truck. Is it all ready?"

Cat said, "Both of the trucks will be finished in the morning."

"All right. On your map you'll see where to park, and at what time. Your two-way radio is for listening only. Set it on the police band and leave it there. When you get my call move fast."

Benson smiled his understanding.

"Cat, you're going to drive the Packard sedan," Frank went on. "It'll be parked in the all-night garage. You'll have to put it in tomorrow morning, then go back when your instructions tell you to. You won't drive it far, but everything else depends on your doing your job properly."

The little man looked annoyed. "Why am I to have the old car?" he asked.

"The instructions explain everything," Frank said.

Cat looked at Hanford questioningly, then back at Frank. He seemed depressed that, after supervising the work on the two trucks, he should be stuck with the wreck of a car. But he nodded at last, accepting the fact.

"Now, there are two O'Farrell Company employees who have to be controlled in order to make the next part of the plan work. One is a guard named Olsen, the other, Kurtz, is the dispatcher for the armored cars. We'll work them in teams—Joe and Cat on the guard, Arnie and Ginther on the dispatcher. There'll be plenty of time after picking them up for those with other assignments at the time of the holdup to get to their posts."

"Where do you fit in?" Joe Hines said.

Cat nodded suddenly. "Yeah. We're in deep enough. You going to watch from safety?"

"Not exactly," Frank said. "As a matter of fact, I plan to be pretty close to the scene of action."

They were all looking at him.

"When the heist begins, I'll be *inside* one of the armored cars!"

After the others had left, taking with them the material's he'd prepared, Frank found he had difficulty raising himself from his chair. The bruised muscles of his body had begun to stiffen again, and he felt faint with pain as he rose. Slowly, he dragged himself into his bedroom. He removed his coat, hunching off the shoulders and letting it drop to the floor. But it hurt too much to bend or turn, and he fell exhausted onto the bed, fully dressed. The aching seemed to course through his body with each pulse-beat of his heart. He closed his eyes against the throbbing and fell into a sort of stupor that was not sleep and was not consciousness. Strange, half-seen dreams invaded his feverish brain.

At first he thought it was another phantom of his imagination, then realized that the girl standing in the doorway to his room was real. He heard her voice, talking to him. Nancy has come back, he thought.

The girl closed the door and moved to the side of his bed. In the dim moonlight from his window, then, he saw the rich billow of dark hair, the deep, luminous eyes. A cheek was pressed wetly to his hand. "Oh, my darling, are you all right? Have they hurt you?" The voice was Vikki's.

He wanted to tell her that he was all right, that she shouldn't be there with him. But the sound he made was only a low moan. She sat on the side of the bed and touched his shoulder. When he flinched she said, "You *are* hurt!"

"No," he whispered. "It's all right. Roughed up a little. I'm okay."

"You're still in your clothes."

He couldn't answer any more. The vague dreaminess seemed to be settling over him once again, and he was no longer sure whether someone was really with him or not. Dimly, he watched as the light in his bathroom flicked on. It glowed out through the open door, illuminating his bed. Vikki appeared with a bottle of something in her hand. She came back to the bed.

"I'm going to take off your things," she told him quietly.

Her fingers worked at his clothing, strong but gentle. As she lifted each shoulder and leg in turn, fresh areas of soreness sent pangs knifing through him. He did not cry out, though. After a while she stopped lifting and turning him, and he knew he lay naked on the bed.

Then the soft coolness began.

Soothingly, he felt the girl's hands on his chest and shoulders, spreading the damp liquid slowly over his body. Each time she touched a bruised area and felt him flinch she stopped and gently kneaded more oil in. Gradually the stretched muscles began to relax; he felt a warm, narcotic drowsiness creeping into his head. The pungent odor of the oil filled his nostrils and seemed to spread a haze in his brain.

He heard her voice, distantly. She was telling him of how she'd worried; how they had been waiting for her that night when she'd come out of her room, on her way to meet him and Fogherty. How they'd locked her in and kept her, refusing to answer her questions about what had happened until she'd gone almost mad for fear that they had killed him. Hanford had relented after Frank came back, taking perverse pleasure in telling her how he'd brought his wife Nancy with him. And how he had played her, Vikki, for a fool. She stopped for a moment, and he knew she was crying. He mumbled something and touched her hand, and she smiled down and continued rubbing him.

For a moment he dozed off, then something woke him again. The light still shone out of the next room, but Vikki was no longer beside him. As though by magic, the pain in his limbs had gone, but he was seized now with a lethargy that seemed almost paralytic. He could not move—or perhaps he could, but something inside him refused to try. He lay motionless, feeling the tingling coolness on his skin from linament, enjoying the deep sense of pleasure and mild excitement that the pressure of the girl's hands had brought.

A shadow fell across his bed and he looked up. Vikki stood there looking down at him. She wore a sheer, russet gown, transparent against the light. The voluptuous curve of her body was silhouetted in the doorway for an instant, then one soft, rounded arm raised, and the light went out.

"Vikki—" he began, but his voice was weak, no more than a whisper. He tensed himself to move, to force her away, but he shuddered at the effort and succeeded only in turning on one side.

He heard the soft rustle of filmy cloth falling to the floor and the brush of a hand near his pillow. Then she was beside him, the warm length of her body caressing his, drawing him close, and he thought, this is insane … it isn't possible … I'll wake up in a moment and have to get up, and—

The sharp intake of breath was a sudden sound in his ear, and he heard her whisper to him, "God, Frank—oh, my darling!"

He slept without stirring, sometimes very deeply, sometimes rising almost to the surface before beginning to sink again. He did not dream any more or did not think he did, though sometimes, when he was nearly awake, he was conscious of the room and of objects around him. It seemed to him Vikki had been there, but once, when he floated up to consciousness, she was not beside him. He was not sure, then, whether she ever had been or not.

Perhaps, he thought, he had imagined it all....

# CHAPTER NINE

WHEN THE DOCTOR CAME into the room it was with the acutely uncomfortable attitude of a man entering a very dark cave in front of which he has just seen bear tracks. He was a somewhat portly little gentleman, dressed as though he'd been ready to leave for the golf course when called. He was wearing tropic-weight linen slacks of a creamy hue, a pleated, open-throat white shirt and a rather well-worn beige-checked jacket, held across his paunch by a single button. Benson followed him into the room and took up a position silently against the door.

Frank was sitting on the edge of the bed with a robe hanging loosely around his shoulders. He had been wakened a few minutes earlier, amazed to learn that it was almost noon. Hanford had told him of the physician's visit—warning against possible treachery—and invited him to join them for lunch as soon as the examination was over. He had managed to get himself to an upright position on the bed, wincing at the rivers of pain that lanced through his chest and sides each time he moved.

"Just check for anything broken," Frank said in a cold voice.

The doctor nodded. "Fine, fine," he said and set to work. Frank clenched his teeth and held on. A few minutes later it was over, and he relaxed. There was a fine film of sweat over his face and chest.

"Nothing out of place. That tape should hold everything together long enough to knit.

"Good."

"You'd best spend the next couple of days in bed, though—or as much time resting as possible."

"Thanks."

The smaller man closed his bag thoughtfully. "Ah—you'll have to be a bit more careful, though, don't you think?"

"That's right, I will."

Giving him a long look, the doctor shrugged slightly, turned and went out. Frank breathed easier. He heard Benson asking how much they owed from the next room. And a moment later the front door closed. Arnie came back into the room.

"Give you a hand dressing," he said.

Frank nodded and let Benson help him into his clothes.

"Look, Frank," the big man said after a moment or two. "This isn't supposed to be my business, and I take no sides, understand?"

Frank glanced toward him, then turned his attention to putting on his tie. "Yeah?"

"It's Jay."

"That isn't news," Frank said. "Hold this coat."

Benson took the jacket and fit it over each arm, pulling it up around Frank's shoulders. "Sure, I know that. But it's a question of timing, if you know what I mean."

"He's got to wait till the job is over with?"

"That's right."

"And afterward?"

Big Arnie made a cutting motion with one finger, perfectly expressing what Ginther had in mind for Frank after the robbery. "If I were you," he said, "I'd find some way to ditch before we get back to the rendezvous."

He nodded. "I see what you mean—thanks, Arnie."

"Don't thank me for anything. You knew all that," the big man said hastily.

Frank smiled. "That's right. I knew all that."

Benson hesitated a moment longer. "I mean, we—well, we worked a lot of jobs together."

He walked over to where the larger man was standing. "Don't worry about it," he said, tapping him on the arm. "I understand."

Arnie looked up, nodded quickly and turned away. "See you tonight, then," he mumbled.

Frank watched him go. He was grateful to Benson, more than the big man knew. Because this answered the one question about which he had not been sure.

Now he knew how Hanford planned to kill him after the hold-up.

A table had been set up outside, on the terrace, and as he came into the front room, he saw Hanford, Vikki, and his wife Nancy sitting around it. With a grimace of annoyance, he went out through the open doors.

"Ah, there you are, Frank. We started without you. Hope you don't mind." Hanford was dressed in his usual black pants and shoes but was without a coat now, his thin, hairless arms protruding from the sleeves of a white linen shirt. Across from him was Vikki, wearing a white terry-cloth robe loosely fastened at the front and cut short above her long, bare legs. Nancy had on a light summer dress in Italian red.

Hanford pointed to the sideboard. "You'll find something to eat there, Frank."

Shelby nodded at him, then smiled toward Nancy. "Hello, darling," he said, "—Vikki." He turned to the side table where several pewter salvers rested with covers over them.

"I fixed it special," Hanford said from behind him. "I hope you like it."

Frank winced to himself. The old man was an excellent chef, but as with all his hobbies, his cooking had a perverse twist: famous last meals. He lifted the covers curiously, looking at each dish. On one tray were several still-hot lamb chops; on another, sweet rolls with butter; in a bowl, fresh-sliced bananas; and, finally, a large pot of hot coffee.

"Whose was this one?" he asked.

"Mr. and Mrs. Borden, of Fall River, Massachusetts," the old man said through a mouthful of food.

Frank took some bananas, covering them with cream from the jug nearby, a roll and a cup of black coffee. Then he came back to the table. "Lizzie's folks?" he asked.

"You're familiar with the case? Served this rather interesting combination to both parents for breakfast before she murdered them with an axe. Very well known. You remember, 'Lizzie Borden took an axe—gave her mother forty whacks,' " he quoted, " '—and when she saw what she had done, gave her father forty-one!' Yes, yes," he chuckled "that's the one. This meal has always interested me."

Nancy looked up at him. "Lamb chops and bananas?" she said.

"It was mutton, actually," Hanford explained, "and *fried* bananas. According to the maid, they had mutton soup with it, also."

"Ugh," Vikki said, putting down her fork.

"Very high in proteins, though," Hanford said, then added "not that it did Mr. and Mrs. Borden much good. But I thought you might like something substantial for tonight, Frank—chops are very energy-giving."

Nancy glanced from her husband, back to the old man. "What's tonight?" she asked.

A short silence answered her; a moment too late, Hanford said, "Why, nothing of any importance, my dear. We're making some final examinations, and there's so little time left we often work in the evening."

Again the silence, and Vikki said, "The pool downstairs is really wonderful, Mrs. Shelby. Perhaps you'd like to join me in a swim a little later."

"Thank you," Nancy murmured, "I'm afraid I haven't a—"

"Oh, I have extra suits, if you'd like to borrow one. That white two-piece of mine should fit—" She looked at Frank: "but it's rather frightfully brief, I suppose—don't you think so, darling?"

The unexpected question surprised him, and he looked up, puzzled.

"How about my knit one for her, you prefer it, don't you?" Vikki turned to the other girl, smiling. "It's a little older, actually, and a bit snug for me, but you're smaller than I am so it should fit about right. Why is it men always like the tight ones?" She laughed.

"I—I don't know," Nancy said, staring with curiosity at the dark-haired girl.

"Well, then, I'll get it," Vikki said, pushing her chair back.

"Uh, maybe Nan doesn't want to go swimming," Frank suggested, glaring meaningfully. It was clear what she was trying to do, and he cursed himself for not having anticipated it.

"Oh, but surely Nancy—" Vikki said. "The men have their stuffy old meeting this afternoon, and you won't want to just sit around. Besides, I see you have a nice tan started, and this'll give you a chance to add to it. Frank always did admire girls with tans," she added.

"Vikki—" he began.

The girl was standing up, loosening her robe. "You must be tired of being cooped up in the city," she told Nancy. "Might as well enjoy the fresh air while you can. You'll find things are ever so much freer and more informal out here, she said, slipping the robe off her shoulders and letting it drop to the chair.

Frank felt as though he had been slapped in the face. For a moment he was not sure whether to laugh or to applaud—the performance had been perfect. Vikki stood before them, two pieces of gauzy green material clinging to her almost naked body. The patch of cloth covering her hips was cut below the soft curve of her belly and laced with a few slender strings at the sides; a narrow band stretched across her breasts, holding them against her chest so tightly that soft mounds of flesh swelled at her armpits and above the straining cloth.

"I'll get something for you," the stunning girl said, no trace of self-consciousness on her face. She started to go, then turned back, her expression thoughtful. "Let me see, now, are those in your room, Frank? Or,—oh, yes, I remember—I have them!" She whirled and ran inside.

They sat in stunned silence. Nancy's face was drained of color. She picked up her fork and absently stirred at the food in her plate. Even Hanford was obviously upset.

The old man cleared his throat. "Ah, I think that, ah—well, you see, Frank and Vikki used to go together, and—that is, a long time ago, and—" he broke off in agitation, realizing he was making matters worse. "I believe I'll excuse myself, now, if you don't mind." He stood and turned to Frank. "I would like to see you in about half an hour. A final check," he added, then bowed shortly and walked away.

"Nan, darling, listen," Frank said. "That was just an act for your benefit. It's true, Vikki and I used to know each other—very well, in fact—but that was before you and I even met."

She looked up at him, her eyes filled with hurt. "And is that why you're staying here now, Frank?"

"No, my God, no!" he cried, shocked. "You know that isn't true!"

She shook her head slowly. "I don't Frank—don't you see? I know so very little about any of this."

"Please try to believe in me, Nan. I'm here because I have to be—because I had no choice in the matter. This involves you as well as me, but I want to protect you from it, darling, I don't want you mixed up in something that was my doing. That's why I can't talk to you about it, but that's the only reason—Vikki has nothing to do with it."

She looked at him steadily, and at last she said, "Do I have your word, Frank? I don't care about the other, but—I couldn't stand this. Do I have your word that there's been—nothing—between you, since you've been here?"

He opened his mouth to speak. And stopped. The memory of the night before floated before him—but that wasn't the same thing, or was it? He had not been in love with Vikki, not ever, not really. . . .

His wife was standing, her face drawn and tight, her lower lip clenched between her teeth. She turned.

"Nancy!"

The girl ran toward his apartment, and he followed her, hurrying inside just as she reached the door to the outer hall.

"*Nancy!* Please, you don't—" The door slammed, and she was gone.

He considered whether or not to go after her, to force her to listen to his explanations—yet, what could he say to her now? How could he make her understand, when he was free to tell only part of the truth? No, it would be better to wait, though it hurt him to know what she must be thinking.

He turned reluctantly from the door and came back down into the room. Vikki was there, standing indecisively, looking out toward the table where a white-jacketed waiter was clearing the luncheon things.

"That was well done," he said bitterly.

She turned and looked at him. "Why, Frank, what do you mean?" Vikki had put on another robe—a full-length, modestly heavy one, fastened securely all the way to her throat. "I was only trying to be hospitable."

"Drop the act, Vikki, you don't need it now."

She walked across to where he was standing. "Act?"

"You know what I mean."

"Yes," she said, "I do. But don't you see? It'll be easier for her this way."

"What are you talking about?"

"Why, that sweet Nancy, your wife. It will be easier if she just sort of sees how things are with you and me. That way it won't be too much of a shock when you tell her."

"How things *are?* What the hell are you—"

"You know," she said smoothly, "how you and I belong here— in a life like this—and how she doesn't. How she could never fit in, not in a million years. Oh, it'll be difficult, even more so for you than for her. But she'll understand—eventually."

He was too startled to reply. Hot, angry words clotted in his throat and stayed there as she leaned close to him, putting her hands on his shoulders. He smelled the dry, clean fragrance of her hair, saw a tiny smile playing at the corners of her full mouth.

"Poor darling," she murmured, "it will be hard for you, won't it? But I know you'll make things right with her. You have such a way of making things right, dear, really you have."

She kissed his mouth with a quick motion, then turned and ran lightly from the room.

He watched in silence as she left, then sat slowly down on the couch.

"My God," he said, and suddenly he knew that he was afraid.

# CHAPTER TEN

I T WAS NOT HIMSELF he was afraid for—it was Nancy. Vikki had hit too close to the truth when she had said, "She doesn't belong here." It was true. Nancy was not one of them, and because she was not, she was dangerous to the gang and to Hanford. In his own case, he might actually have pressured Hanford into letting him go after the holdup, each confident the other would have to keep silent. But with Nancy it was different. The old man had no guarantees with her—she was a threat to him as long as she lived.

As long as she lived . . . .

With sudden decision, he started back to Hanford's quarters. The old man admitted him as soon as he knocked.

"I did not expect you quite so soon, Frank."

"Things broke up kind of fast out front," he said.

"I'm sorry, my boy, that was certainly uncalled for, I'll agree. I'll speak to Vikki if you like."

Frank shook his head. "No need for it now. It'll all be over in a few hours anyway."

"Yes, yes of course. That's why I asked you to come in, in fact. The time is growing near, and I wanted to be certain everything was arranged to your satisfaction."

"There are a couple of points," Frank said.

"Fine, what are they?"

"First of all, someone is going to have to drive the big truck down to the rendezvous—that old shed near the dump that Arnie checked out. The one we used to use."

"I remember. I can take care of that, if there's nothing more to it."

"That's all," Frank said. "Just drive it there and wait for us. The second thing is that I need a small machine-type screwdriver—something I can work on a gun action with."

Hanford nodded. "I'll ask Arnie to get it for you. Is that all?"

Frank hesitated a moment, then said, "Not quite. There's one thing more. About our arrangements, yours and mine. They aren't quite satisfactory as they stand at the moment."

Hanford raised his eyebrows. "Oh? In what way?"

"I'm not happy with having Nancy involved in this. I want to see her out."

The old man shrugged. "You can hardly blame me, Frank. It was your idea to force my hand."

"Nothing I did made it all right for you to kidnap my wife, Hanford. Let's not get confused."

"That's a good idea, my boy," the other said, turning an acute gaze on him. "Let's not get confused. Let's not forget that 'right' or 'wrong' have very little to do with this at the moment. We will each of us do what we have to—and you have to do as I say. Otherwise..." He smiled and tilted his little bald head to one side. "Otherwise you will suffer for it, and so will your wife."

Frank appeared to be considering the old man's words carefully. They were about what he had expected and prepared for. Deliberately, he pulled a package of cigarettes from his pocket, shook one loose and took it between his lips. He reached over to the desk for the lighter lying there, then glanced up into the old man's face. "I don't think so," he said.

"What?"

Frank shook his head. "No, I don't really think so.... I don't think you'd let all this go down the drain, just to keep my wife handy."

"I warn you, Frank—"

"No, don't warn me, listen to me. You wouldn't even start to do something to Nan—torture her, or anything like that, not at this point. Because you know what it would do to the men. You know they're edgy already—something like this, and they would blow sky-high. Your whole scheme would fold."

The small man was silent now, a deep scowl distorting his countenance.

"At least, that is what I'm betting on, Hanford—I've thought everything over very carefully, and I'm ready to go all the way."

There was a moment's silence—then, "Just what is it you want?"

Frank relaxed a little inside. His face remained impassive. "I want positive assurances that Nancy will be turned loose after this job is finished."

"If we are successful, as soon as we return—"

Shelby was shaking his head slowly. "Uh-uh. That won't get it. She's got to be set free the minute the job is completed—before any of us return here."

"How do you propose we accomplish that?" the other asked.

"I've thought about that, too," Frank said.

"And—"

"I'll trust Vikki to handle it."

"Vikki? How?"

"You will lock Nancy into her room before we leave, is that right?" Frank said.

The old man nodded.

"All right. Vikki gets the key to that room. As soon as we've pulled the job, we call her—either you or I—and tell her to turn Nancy loose." He paused. "Those are my conditions."

Mr. Hanford sat thinking a moment, then said, "You're clever, Frank, a very clever man."

"That's why I'm here."

"Exactly. Very well, I agree to your proposal. I warn you, though, there are to be no tricks."

"You took the words right away from me," Frank said.

"Incidentally, how do you know Miss Porter will be willing to assist you in your little plan?"

Frank smiled wearily. "I have a hunch that Vikki isn't any more anxious to have Nan here than I am—only for different reasons."

Hanford nodded slowly. "Yes, I suppose you may be right. Very well, how will you make the arrangements?"

"I'll talk to Vikki, get her to agree. Before we leave, then, I want to see the key to Nancy's room actually worked in the lock, then I want to see you give it to Vikki."

The little old man stood up slowly. "That will be just before midnight, then."

"Yes."

"Very good. I shan't bother you again until tonight, in that case," Hanford said coldly.

Frank stood also.

Hanford looked up at him, then said, "Ordinarily, Frank, I do not allow myself to be dictated to, especially on the terms you've chosen. In this case, of course, where your wife is involved—" He shrugged. "Well, I can understand that you would go to unusual lengths. But let me tell you, my boy, you would be ill-advised ever again to try such tactics on me."

The small man came out from behind his desk and opened the door for Frank. "I think you understand," he said as Frank went past. "Good-by."

Frank walked out into the hall and heard the door shut behind him. A shudder ran through his body—the kind one feels after watching death pass very close.

He went back to his room and sat down heavily on the sofa. He looked at his watch. The hours would go quickly now, even though it was just mid-afternoon. He felt exhausted already, and the idea of the night ahead seemed to sap his strength. He stretched out on the couch, letting his painfully taped body relax a little, hoping to conserve himself as much as possible. The instant he did so a crowd of thoughts seemed to spring from the dark corners of his brain, clamoring for attention. He fought them back, refusing to answer: What about Vikki...? How can you be sure Nancy is safe...? When will Ginther try for you...? And, most of all, what about the "idea"—the plan that has taken form in the hours just past and that is demanding recognition now?

At six o'clock he woke up, oppressed by a feeling of impending doom. He lit a cigarette and sat smoking it to calm his nerves. He told himself everything was going to be all right. He knew it was a lie.

Shrugging off the swarm of doubts that had returned to plague him, he got up and went to the telephone, ordered dinner sent up to his room and went in to shower. The food arrived just as he finished shaving, and he ate hurriedly before getting dressed. There were still several last-minute details to be considered in the time that remained. First, he had to see Vikki to ask her help, and it was not a meeting he looked forward to.

He glanced at his watch. The others would be started on their ways by now; Joe Hines and Cat to the home of Olsen, the guard; Ginther and Big Arnie to pick up the man named Kurtz. After securing the two O'Farrell men, Cat and Benson would hurry to take up their positions for later that night, while Hines remained with the guard and Ginther went with Kurtz. It was all planned smoothly. He hoped it was all going smoothly.

He knotted his tie swiftly, adjusting it in the mirror behind the bar, then turned and picked up the phone again. He was surprised to discover that he had become quite calm.

"Ring Miss Porter for me, please," he said.

A moment later Vikki's voice said, "Hello?"

"This is Frank."

"Oh, hello," she said more warmly.

"I want to talk to you for a few minutes, can I?"

"Certainly, shall I come over, or—"

"I can find you, I guess."

"All right, I'll let you in. It's on the right at the end of the hall."

"Fine. I'm coming down now." He hung up and went over to the white door near the aquarium. He heard the rasp of the magnetic lock and pushed inward. The door opened.

The hallway was identical to the one leading to Hanford's suite except that, at the end of it, was a full-length mirror. Another person seemed to be walking toward Frank as he approached. Doors flanked the mirror on either side, the right hand one standing partially open.

"Come in," Vikki called to him.

The room was small by comparison with Frank's, expensively furnished in simple taste and not particularly feminine-looking. The entire right-hand wall faced out onto the terrace and, though he had not noticed it from outside, was made of one-way glass. The light, flickering in through the open curtains, gave the room a bluish tint and accented the whites and blacks of the walls and furniture.

Vikki was at the small rattan bar in the far corner of the room, fixing two drinks. "What was that classic line that the spider gave the fly?" she asked.

Frank smiled. "Whatever it was, he could have saved his breath—if the fly was already in the web."

The girl came out from behind me bar with the glasses. She was wearing a pair of tight-fitting toreador pants cut to the widest point of her well-shaped calves, a simple, white cotton blouse with the front only half buttoned, and a half-dollar-sized silver medallion suspended on a silver link chain. The medallion glowed against her smooth skin, making it look dark in the blue light. Her feet were bare, a pair of turquoise slippers lying carelessly on the floor in front of the sofa. She looked cool and lithe in the outfit and moved as gracefully through the filtered light of the room as an underwater creature. Frank thought of old man Hanford's aquarium outside, and of man-eating fish ....

"Stop looking as though you really believed that 'spider and fly' business." She smiled at him. "Here, take this and grab a chair—better yet, join me." She sat down on the sofa and patted the cushion beside her.

"Maybe I'd better tell you why I've come first," he said.

The girl shrugged. "All right, meeting will come to order."

"This is pretty serious," he said.

Her face sobered. "Serious," she said, "now I'm very serious."

He walked closer to where she was sitting and looked down. "I want you to do me a favor—not an easy one, but one which means a great deal to me."

She returned his gaze without answering.

"I want you to help Nancy," he said.

Vikki's look was one of mild surprise, then puzzlement. She drew her legs up beside her on the couch and tilted her head a bit to one side. "Let me have a cigarette," she said, "then sit down and tell me what you're talking about. I won't throw you out—just yet."

The girl's tone was still light, though with a slight edge to it now. He pulled a package of cigarettes from his pocket and held it out. She took one, bending her head forward for a light, the long hair falling along both sides of her lovely, high-boned face. She looked up at him from veiled eyes and brushed her hair back.

"Just how am I supposed to help your wife—providing I wanted to?"

"I've arranged it all with Hanford. He's agreed, as long as it's all right with you. After we leave here tonight, you'll be by yourself—Nancy will be locked in her room. You're to have the key to that room. When Hanford or I call, after the job is finished, you are to unlock her and help her get away."

She studied his face through the thin haze of cigarette smoke. "Sounds easy. Why all the cloak and dagger?"

He shrugged. "I don't trust Hanford. I want to make sure he doesn't double-cross me, and I want to be certain Nancy gets clear of this business."

"What makes you think I can do it?"

He looked puzzled. "What do you mean?"

"Supposing Stanley tells me to pretend to agree but to leave the door closed till he gets back?"

"Then you'd have to act on your own. But remember, I'll be here—nobody will bother you."

"Will you be?" the girl raised her eyebrows, smiling. "I had wondered about that. ... What do you say we make a little deal on that?"

Frank waited.

"I'll do what you want," she said, "but only on one condition. And if you're a good guesser, maybe you know what that is." Vikki pressed out her cigarette in the ashtray at her arm, then turned toward him on the couch.

"It's that after this job is finished, you don't go back to her, Frank—that you stay here with me. Like it used to be."

He didn't answer immediately, and she watched his face for some response. "Don't be a fool, darling. You can't go back, you must realize that—Stanley would never allow you for one thing, and then, it's, well—too late."

"Too late for what?" he said.

"Too late for you to be anything other than what you are," she answered evenly.

He met her eyes a moment, then looked away. Why not admit it? he asked himself. She's pegged it for you. ... She knows as well as you do that it's all over so far as Nancy is concerned. All you can do for her, now, is get her out of the mess you've made—if you can—and then get out of her life for good.

Absently, he picked up a cigarette and held it in his fingers. It was stupid to have ever thought he could break away—be something he wasn't. This was all he was good for, and it wasn't much, but he could at least make the best of it while he lasted. Yes, he could do that, he thought.

Aloud, he said, "All right, Vikki. That's how it will be."

She moved toward him on the couch, kneeling and putting both her hands on his shoulders, looking into his face. "It's best, Frank, please believe me it is. I'll try so hard to make you happy, darling—I will, really."

"And you'll do as I asked you tonight?"

"Yes," she whispered, "no matter what."

"All right, then. I have to go, but I'll see you again before we leave."

"Do you—have to?" she said, her voice low and appealing.

"I'm afraid so," he said.

"But you'll be back—"

He bent and kissed her lightly, then turned and went out of the room.

The telephone was ringing frantically as he came back into his apartment. He hurried to answer it, noticing in passing that Benson had been there; the small metal screwdriver he'd asked for rested on the bar-top. He slipped it into his pocket and picked up the phone. It was Hanford. The little man's voice came out piercingly, shrill with agitation.

"It's Hines!" he cried. "The fool has ruined everything!"

"*Hold it, hold it!* What's wrong?"

"He's let the guard escape!" the old man raged. "Our plans are destroyed—do you understand? Olsen has eluded him, and everything is *finished!*"

# CHAPTER ELEVEN

Now TAKE IT EASY, for God's sake!" Frank said. Hanford was pacing furiously, spitting out anger and frustration. "There may be a way out of this," he said.

The old man whirled. "Do you think—"

Frank made an annoyed gesture with one hand. "I don't think anything yet—I've got a hunch, that's all, and I can't work it out right because you're making so much fuss."

"All right, all right!" Hanford cried. He clasped his hands and sat down. For several moments he remained silent, then, able to contain himself no longer, he jumped up again. "We'll do it without the guard, then," he cried. "Jay can force the dispatcher to make the substitution and get you in the truck."

"That's just fine," Frank snapped. "What would Olsen have to say about that after reporting for work? You'd have a scene right there at the O'Farrell office and we'd be in trouble."

"Then what are we going to do?"

"Give me your car keys," Frank said.

"What?"

"I'll need the car for about an hour, maybe two. If I handle this myself I may be able to straighten it out." He saw the suspicious look on Hanford's face and headed him off. "You can stand around arguing with me, if you like, or you can do as I say and hope I'm lucky. Make up your mind, because we haven't got much time." He turned and started for the bedroom. "Have the car brought around front," he said over his shoulder to the startled Hanford. "Then get me a line out. I've got to make a phone call."

Frank went into his room and picked a coat from the closet. Outside, he could hear the old man speaking reluctantly into the telephone. When he came back into the living room, Hanford gloweringly passed the instrument to him.

"Thanks." Frank placed his body between Hanford and the phone and dialed a number quickly.

"I needn't remind you, I'm sure, that your wife will suffer if this is some sort of trick."

"That's right," Frank said, "you needn't."

The ringing continued long and unbroken. Frank felt his heart sinking. Then at last there was a sharp click, and a woman's voice said, "Hello?"

"This is Frank Shelby," he said quickly. "Do you remember me?"

There was a pause on the line. The voice was no longer sleepy-sounding. "Yes, I remember you."

"I want to see you—it's very important. I think I can help you."

"What do you mean?" The voice was hard and suspicious.

"I can't tell you on the phone. That's why I want to see you."

"I don't understand. Why don't you say what you want?"

"Someone is listening," he told her.

There was another pause. "When?" she asked finally.

"Now. You'll understand why when I see you. But this is urgent. Tomorrow will be too late."

"But—"

"Please, if you want me to help it will have to be now."

"Well—"

"I'll be there in thirty minutes—no—" He looked at his watch—"in twenty-five. Good-by." He hung up and turned to see Hanford's eyes measuring him carefully.

"The car keys," he said.

Reluctantly, the old man handed them over, then walked to the door with him. "You have until twelve, midnight—two and

one-half hours," Hanford said. "If you are not back by then—"
The two men's eyes met for an instant. Frank turned without
answering and started down the hall.

The car was waiting in front of the club. It was a dark green
Mercedes 300S. Sparse touches of polished chrome accented its
handsome, well-bred lines. The lot attendant held the door for
him as he slid in over the soft leather seats, smelling the rich odor
of animal hide and hand-rubbed wood. The door closed behind
him with a clump.

"You'll have to put 'er away yourself when you get back," the
attendant told him through the window. "Club's closed tonight.
I'm off now."

Frank nodded. "All right," he said. He put the car in gear and
pulled away, feeling the silent surge of power from the engine as
he swung up onto the highway and accelerated toward town.

He hoped he would not have too much trouble finding the
house. He had seen it once before, and it hadn't seemed too difficult to reach. He wondered what he would say when he got
there, whether he could make his story convincing enough. And,
finally, most importantly, whether or not Sandy Fogherty would
be willing to help him when he did find her.

The house was dark and silent when he arrived and walked
up to the front porch. At first his knock went unanswered, then
the peep-hole in the door slid open and someone looked out at
him.

"It's me," he said. "May I come in?"

The door opened slowly to reveal the figure of a girl dressed
in a faded robe, her hair disarrayed. He stepped quickly inside.

"Couldn't this have waited?" she asked again.

He shook his head. "No, it couldn't. We have to talk now."

"Is it about—Jim?" She seemed to pronounce the name
with difficulty. He saw that she was confused, almost dazed
still, and realized how the big man's death must have shocked
her.

"Yes," he said, "in a way, it is. I'm sorry, Sandy, I really am."

"Who did it?" she said. "Who killed him?" Her voice was flat, automatic.

"Can we sit down?" he asked.

Sandy looked around distractedly, brushing at a loose strand of hair across her cheek. "Excuse me, I—come in, won't you? Would you like some coffee?"

"All right," he said. He didn't want the coffee, but letting her steady her obviously taut nerves at the small task seemed a good idea. They moved into the kitchen, and she switched on a single, overhead light. He saw her face clearly for the first time, and it startled him—pale and drawn, deep lines of anguish etched into the features that had been so vivid and young the last time he'd seen them. Was it possible, he wondered, that she could have cared for him that much? For the hundredth time, he cursed Fogherty for having been a fool.

"Would you rather have some fresh?" she asked him, bringing a pot from the stove. "I made this right after you called."

"This is fine."

She brought cream and sugar and put it on the table, then stood, looking about as though something were missing—something forgotten. The expression of distraction in her eyes hurt him.

"Please," he said, "please sit down."

Slowly, she sank into the chair and pressed her hands against her eyes. "I'm tired," she said. "I guess I haven't quite accepted it all yet." She looked up at him suddenly, and for the first time there was a hint of fear in her face.

"What is it?" she said. "Why have you come here?"

"I came to help," he told her. "Listen, Sandy, I didn't have anything to do with the death of your husband—except that I tried to prevent it and almost got myself killed as well."

For the first time she seemed to notice the bruises on his face. She frowned and nodded.

"I'm against them, and I came here tonight because I'd hoped you were, too."

She studied his eyes for a long moment, then something inside her seemed to relax. "Do you know how it happened?"

He nodded. "Yes, I know."

Her face twisted in anguish. "Why did they do it?" she cried. "Why?"

He didn't speak, didn't touch her. He let her cry, because he knew whatever he said wouldn't help. After a while she stopped. She dried her face on her sleeve.

"Would—you like—some more coffee?" she said, fumbling a handkerchief from her pocket. She smiled self-consciously. "Please don't mind me," she said. "I'll be all right."

He leaned forward to the girl, looking intently at her. He was sure now that it was going to be all right—that she would listen to him. Now was the time to tell her.

"I'm going to cross the gang, Sandy," he said, quietly but with emphasis. "The transfer is tonight, and I'm going to pull a double-cross—make the robbery backfire. The men who killed Jim will pay for what they've done—if you'll help me."

Her eyes widened in surprise, and for a moment he was seized with sudden doubt—what if he had guessed wrong? What if she didn't believe him or refused to help? Would he take her back to the Xanadu with him to prevent her calling the police? It was too late, he knew, to change his plans. He sat tensely, waiting. At last she answered.

"Thank you, Frank," she whispered. "Oh, thank you." Her eyes were fevered with hope. "Yes, God, yes—I'll help. I'll do anything you ask!"

It was nearing eleven o'clock when he pulled down into the parking lot in front of the club once again. He had telephoned from the Fogherys' house with instructions, and now Hanford was in a near frenzy of nervous agitation.

"What happened?" he demanded the instant Frank walked into the room. "Is it going to be all right? Tell me what this is all about!"

"Did you tell Joe to call as soon as he knew about the guard?" Frank asked.

"Yes, yes, of course. But what is he doing at the Fogherty woman's place? What has she to do with all this?"

"That's easy—she's the bait. I figured that, since the men in the two companies knew each other, Sandy probably knew some of the wives. She did. So I had her phone Mrs. Olsen and find out where her husband was."

The old man's thin brows shot up. "Ahh—" he said.

"It worked fine. Mrs. Olsen was there, and Sandy found that her husband had left early to have dinner and spend some time at the Elks Club before going to work."

"Wasn't Olsen's wife suspicious?"

"I had Sandy tell her the same thing she told Olsen when she found him—that something had come up about Jim's death and that she had to see him right away. She stressed that no one else must know about it and that she couldn't answer any more questions on the phone."

"And he fell for it?"

"Why not? He knew Sandy, knew that there was something fishy about Jim's death. Olsen was a cop, of sorts, and he figured it was his business—it was natural for Sandy to call someone she knew. Besides which, Mrs. Fogherty happens to be quite an attractive woman—the kind most men would like to aid in distress."

"I see," Hanford said with a slight smile. "But how did you ever get her to do this for you, Frank?"

"Like I said, she's *very* attractive—and I've known her for some time, you know." He hated himself for the lie, feeling ashamed and squirmy as he uttered it, but knowing that it was important Hanford believe him.

He did. The little man nodded with obvious pleasure, swallowing the implication whole. Frank had been sure he would, simply because it was so much the sort of thing the old man *liked* to believe in—Frank betraying the dead Fogherty with his own wife, at the same time bargaining for Vikki and Nancy. Yes, that was Hanford's dish, all right. He was probably already looking for some souvenir of it to add to his collection of oddities. Frank resisted an urge to strike the smirking little mouth.

"You are a wonder, my boy, truly you are."

Shelby turned away quickly, afraid of what might show in his face. "I'd like to see my wife now, before we go," he said.

The old man nodded. "Of course." He took out a key and, smiling, gave it to Frank. "You know the room?"

"Yes," Frank said and started for the door. Before he could reach it the phone rang.

Hanford rushed to answer it. "Yes?" he said. "Yes, yes, this is he! What?" A slow grin spread across the icy features. The small, hard eyes flickered across to Frank, and slowly the little man's head moved up and down. "Excellent! Very good. You know what to do now? All right. Yes—good-by!"

Hanford replaced the phone and looked at Frank in triumph. "It was Joe! He has Olsen!"

Frank glanced at his watch. "We'll leave in twenty minutes, then."

He went out of the room and down the hall to Nancy's apartment. There for an instant he hesitated, calling on his courage. This was going to be difficult, probably, yet so much depended on its going right. He had to handle it just so. At last he raised his hand and knocked. A muffled voice from inside answered.

"Who is it?"

"Me—Frank. I'd like to talk to you."

He heard footsteps crossing the room quickly. "Frank?" The voice was tense, a note of eagerness in it.

"Yes, darling, I'd like to come in—just for a minute."

"Oh, Frank!" she cried. "It's locked!"

"I have a key." He opened the door, and Nancy was suddenly in his arms, crying happily.

"Oh, my darling, I was so afraid you wouldn't come. I was so frightened that you'd go without letting me see you, tell you how sorry I—" Her words choked off into sobs.

He pushed the door closed and stood holding her to him. "Nan, darling, don't cry—please don't," he said, relieved and happy. She was no longer angry.

Nancy led him into the room, a small apartment compared to the others he'd seen in the building, clean and newly furnished. There were no windows, and apparently only the one door exiting onto the hall. They sat together on the couch, Nancy still holding his hand tightly.

"It was silly, darling. I don't know what came over me," she said. "I—I guess I was still upset over the night before, and it was so strange because everyone was acting as if things were perfectly normal, and of course I knew they weren't. I guess I was just nervous and afraid and—and *mad* inside, and I took it all out on you!"

"Don't feel bad about it—I understand. You had every reason. God, what a shock all this must have been—be," he said sadly. She came to him, and they kissed, the taste of tears still on her mouth.

"Frank, I'm so glad you're here," she whispered. "I wanted you to hold me like this so much!" She rubbed her face deeper into his shoulder.

He remembered the things he'd come to tell her then, and was conscious of how little time remained. The pain in him now was not of his bruised body alone—it was a stronger, more despairing kind. As though sensing his disturbance, Nancy lifted her head and looked into his face.

"You're going to go soon," she said, not questioning.

"Yes."

She spoke very quietly. "You came to say good-by?"

"I wanted to be sure you were all right."

"I am," she said. Her voice was stronger. "I've had a lot of time to think, today—since this morning."

"Yes."

"About you and me—everything here."

"None of it was your fault, Nan, it was all me."

"These men—they're criminals, aren't they?" she said. "There's going to be some sort of robbery tonight, isn't there? And you're going to be part of it."

He sat stunned—knowing that he should not be, knowing that she would have been stupid not to have guessed most of it. Yet he was reluctant to believe that at last she knew the truth in spite of everything.

She sat watching him, and his eyes told her the answer to her question. "I thought that was it," she said quietly. "After this morning I was almost sure. And then, of course, I realized why you wouldn't tell me anything. I knew that this must have been the part of your life that you had hidden from me—ever since the beginning."

"I'm sorry about it all, Nan," he said.

She shook her head. "Don't be sorry for this, Frank. You see, I never would have minded if you'd told me. I might have loved you more, knowing what you'd been through, or perhaps it wouldn't have made any difference at all. I don't know. All I knew is that you should have told me, Frank. That's all there is to be sorry for."

"I know that now." He nodded and suddenly it was true. He knew that his real mistake had been in not telling Nancy the truth, in not trusting her love enough and in failing to believe that she could love him as he did her.

"Did you think I wouldn't have forgiven you?"

He looked away. "Yes," he said. "I ran, you see, I was afraid. I didn't have the courage to fight, and I didn't have the guts to risk losing you."

"Then stop now, darling. Stop and fight them."

"No," he said. "Not now."

"No matter what it means, Frank, I'd rather that than see you go with them and help them tonight."

He closed his eyes a moment, then opened them again, looking at her. "I'm going tonight," he said, "—but not to help them."

He saw realization dawn slowly in his wife's eyes, and he saw the growing horror there.

"Frank, no!" she gasped. "Please, Frank, what are you doing?" She stood suddenly, and he jumped up too. "God, you mustn't, oh, Frank, stay with me please!"

He caught her shoulders as she struggled, drawing his arms down around her, pinning her twisting body to his and holding her so hard that his taped ribs burned under the weight. Slowly the breath was forced out of her, until she clung helplessly to him.

"*Listen … listen … listen!*" he whispered over and over into her ear. At last she was silent, rigid as marble, gripping him relentlessly with her small hands.

"Can you understand me, Nancy, will you listen to what I'm saying?" He was calm, knowing what he had to do. The watch on his wrist, visible over the girl's shoulder, told him Hanford was due. His time was up—he had to tell her. Slowly, he shook the girl back and forth. "Will you listen?" he said again.

"Yes," she breathed.

"This is for me, Nan, not just for you. How could I live otherwise, with or without you, if I didn't do this?" He felt her begin to tremble in his arms.

"I don't want to die, Nancy, but more than that, I won't want to live unless I can make it right again. Mostly, it's you and me, but my whole life has shaped this moment, and if I turn back— and live—I'll spend the rest of it like a frightened animal. I've got to do this or nothing has any meaning any more."

She was crying hard against his shoulder, great sobs tearing up from somewhere deep inside—but she cried almost silently, not resisting, listening to his voice, and he knew that she understood now.

"I want you to remember what I'm telling you, darling," he said, pressing his lips against her cheek. "You must remember, no matter what happens to me. Remember that it was all right, no matter what, it was all right then."

There was a sharp knock at the door.

"Just a minute," he said loudly.

Nancy stirred in his arms, her sobs dying away. When a moment later she pulled back a little, he saw that she was not crying. He smiled down at her. "You'll be released after a while," he said, "after we're gone. I want you to go home, Nancy. I want you to go back to Blaine."

Again the pounding came from the door. She moved toward him, and they kissed once more, long and deep, a kiss of good-by. She touched his cheek with one hand and then drew her hand away. For a moment longer they stood, then he turned and went to the door.

"All right, Hanford," he said.

Frank stepped out into the hall, closing the door behind him and locking it again. Then he stood facing the old man. "Let's go." They started down the hall. "Where's Vikki?" Frank asked.

"In your room," Hanford said.

Frank went in, leaving the other man to wait in the hall. Vikki was sitting at the bar, sipping a drink. He nodded at her, not speaking, and went into his room. Quickly, he changed into the guard's uniform, then put on an overcoat, checked the pocket to be sure he had the small screwdriver Benson had got him and went back into the living room again.

"You know what to do with this?" he said to the girl, handing her the key to Nancy's apartment.

"I know."

He nodded. "I'll see you—afterward."

# CHAPTER TWELVE

THE BIG GREEN MERCEDES cruised through the night, its broad headlight beams cutting a path out of the darkness.

"Nervous, are you, Frank?" the little man said, glancing over from the driver's seat.

"A little."

Shelby was conscious of a heightened awareness of himself and the things about him—the cold smell seeping in from outside and mingling with the sharp leather odor of the seats, the strange tightness of his uniform and the irritating pressure of rough wool on the skin of his wrists and neck, the sick, sinking feeling in his stomach.

It would be misty in New York. Lights shown against the thickening clouds in an aurora, spreading shroudlike across the giant corpse of the city.

"You won't have any trouble finding the shed when you take the carrier down?" Frank asked.

"None at all. I remember the place quite well."

"You may get stopped.... A big truck like that is a damn funny-looking thing to be driving around a deserted part of town at midnight."

"I own a car lot, officer," Hanford mimicked his excuse, "and I was supposed to pick up a couple of junkers down here earlier. But I got lost."

Frank nodded. "Not good, but it's something to say. Better hope nobody asks."

"Don't worry," the little man said softly, "I'll manage this part of it."

They were picking up streetlights and the fronts of factory buildings now, plunging into the outskirts of the city. Hanford cut off the main highway and began to thread down deserted side-streets.

"We should get there by 12:45, don't you think?" Hanford said.

"Maybe earlier, at this rate."

"I'll go more slowly."

When they crossed over at the George Washington Bridge, Hanford pulled the car up so that Frank had to reach out and pay the toll. For a while they drove in silence, and then the old man said, "We were lucky that Mrs. Fogherty co-operated."

Frank nodded, noticing that they seemed to be running into more fog now, thinking that would be a break too. "Too bad about Jim," he said, "even if he did bring it on himself."

"He did?" Hanford said.

"Tipping you to my plans the night I flew back to Blaine, I mean. You probably know I offered to let him go with me."

"Yes," the old man said, "I know." There was a strange note in his voice. "But, of course, it wasn't Jim who told me what you were going to do."

Frank heard the words dimly, through his thoughts, then came abruptly alert to them. He had a sudden, dawning premonition. Almost before the old man spoke again, Frank knew what Hanford was going to say.

"It was Vikki who told me." Hanford smiled. "I rather thought you would have figured that out by now."

"Vikki!"

"Certainly, my boy—but you mustn't think she meant to harm you. In fact, she was very insistent that you be kept safe. Jay's leaving you where the police could find you was his idea."

Thoughts spun through Frank's head. He tried to calm himself and to make sense of this new knowledge. How did it affect what he had to do? What warning did it hold for him? But he could not concentrate. He could think of only one thing—*what about Nancy?*

Hanford was peering out of the windshield into the thickening fog. "This is where we turn, isn't it?"

The Mercedes approached the corner swiftly, slowed a little, swinging around, then began to pick up speed rapidly as Hanford fed gasoline to the powerful motor. The speedometer needle leaped upward as they flashed past the front of the O'Farrell Building, then began to slow again. The big car pulled into the curb with astonishing nimbleness and stopped.

"Just in case Jay had failed, I didn't want us to step into a trap," Hanford said. "Everything looked all right, though." He left the motor running.

Frank checked his wristwatch and saw that they were on time. It's too late to change anything now, he thought. Your only hope—and Nancy's—is to make this work... then the rest won't matter.

He opened the door and stepped out. "I'll see you, then," he said.

"Be careful," Hanford told him. The big green car moved away from the curb, accelerating rapidly to the next corner. It turned—and was gone.

Frank felt suddenly chilled and unsure. What if Ginther *had* failed—what if they were just waiting for him now? Shrugging off the thought, he began walking toward the light. At the doors he paused and looked inside. Everything appeared normal, several people were at their desks or moving about the large office. He grasped the handle firmly and turned. It resisted the pressure of his hand. The door was locked. He stood a moment, surprised and confused, then saw a girl moving toward him, attracted by the rattle of the lock. He fought a desire to run and stood stiffly as she unfastened the catch and pushed the door open a crack.

"Yes?"

"Nolan, from Van Ness Company," he said. "I'm relief tonight."

The girl didn't answer. She stepped back, allowing him to enter. He passed her, and the door was locked again behind him. "Mr. Kurtz is in his office—to the left, at the end of the corridor," the girl said. She glanced at him incuriously through eyes made colder by thick glasses. She was plainly dressed, with a look of forbidding efficiency about her.

He stood a moment longer, unfastening his overcoat, taking advantage of the pause to survey the O'Farrell Company office. It was a large room, somewhat like a bank lobby, two storys high with only the back half of the upper level built over. Two windows faced out over the heads of the people below. The feeling that he might be watched from one of these sent a quick shiver over him. He shook the coat out across one arm and started for the dispatcher's office.

The short corridor ended in a big wooden door with red lettering across the top—GARAGE AREA—AUTHORIZED PERSONNEL ONLY. To the right was a self-service elevator and, a few feet back from it, a staircase. The frosted glass door on the left read: HENRY KURTZ, DISPATCHER. He lifted his hand to knock, then let it drop. He turned the handle and pushed forward.

As he came through the door, he flashed a glance around, seeing the room in a flat, dimensionless picture as he had learned to do—taking in all details at once, uncritically and inclusively, senses alert to pick out the first incongruous feature or movement.

He saw a double-sized office with two desks at the far end of the room, a girl at one of the desks, next to another door leading to the garage area, and a man seated facing him who must be Kurtz, coat on, a shock of iron-colored hair looking uncombed and fierce. And he saw Ginther, legs crossed, hands folded near the opening of his coat, just above his belt. There was something wrong—*what?*

Frank's eyes swung quickly back to the man at the big desk—something in his face, he could see it quite clearly now—a steely excitement, a tense readiness. Ginther was a fool! This man was waiting for Frank.

Kurtz had straightened in his chair, his eyes glittering with apprehension as Frank approached, his fingertips brushing the top edge of his desk, ready to drop out of sight.

"Bill Nolan, I believe," Kurtz said, "from the Van Ness Company?"

Frank leaned forward with his hands on the dispatcher's desk. "I've just come from your house," he said in a low voice. "Your family is perfectly all right. There's nothing to worry about!"

The man with the gray hair froze, a softening of the muscles around mouth and eyes indicating his shock. From the corner of his vision Frank could see Ginther's puzzled face.

"What—what do you mean?" Kurtz muttered at last.

"Just that everything is going to be fine—so long as you don't reach for what you've got in that drawer. Then everything won't be so fine—for you or your family."

The dispatcher leaned back slowly in his seat, the muscles of his body sagging. Ginther seemed to understand what Frank had done now. He leaned closer to the other man and said, "That's okay, Mac, you act nice and you got nothing to worry about."

Frank saw that the girl at the other end of the room was looking at them with curiosity. Still in a low voice, he turned to Kurtz again and said, "Look natural—we don't want anybody getting upset." The dispatcher followed his glance. Slowly, he sat up again, seeming to force renewed strength into himself. Frank couldn't help admiring the man.

"Miss Peters," Kurtz said loudly. The girl stood up. "Have you put Mr. Nolan down for relief tonight?"

"Yes, sir," the girl said. "I'll need some social security information, though."

Frank whispered, without moving his lips, "It's getting
late—tomorrow."

"Well, I think we can fill that in in the morning," Kurtz told
her. "It's about time to leave now."

"Yes, sir," the girl said and sat down at her desk.

"All right," Frank said. "Let's get this over with."

Kurtz looked at him fearfully and stood up, his mouth drawn
into a tight line. "If you harm—"

"Shut up," Frank told him quietly and looked toward Ginther.
"Try to keep back out of the way when we're in the garage, will
you?" he said to the blond-haired man. Then he turned to Kurtz.
"Move. You've got some guns here." He knew that a man like this
understood professionalism. Kurtz knew enough about holdup
men to know which ones were deadly and which were not. He
wanted Kurtz to get the right idea about them.

The dispatcher stepped to a wooden cabinet and unlocked it
with a key from the chain on his belt. Inside were rows of guns
and ammunition. Frank stepped forward. "What am I riding?"
he said.

"Shotgun," Kurtz answered, aware that Frank already knew
the answer to the question.

"What are they carrying—and don't try to kid me."

The dispatcher hesitated, then pointed to one end of the rack.

Ginther gave a low whistle from behind them. "Thompsons,
huh?"

Frank pulled down one of the short, ugly submachine
guns and turned it in his hands. Its dark metal was oily to his
touch, heavy and ungainly. He pulled out a drawer below the
rack and selected several loaded clips. He slipped them into
the pockets of his uniform, then nodded for Kurtz to close the
case. Together the three men moved for the door at the rear of
the office.

"The trucks are due out in exactly—" Kurtz looked at his watch—"ten minutes, Miss Peters. If I have any calls, hold them."

The girl nodded, smiled at the other men and went back to her work. Kurtz opened the door and motioned for them to follow. A short flight of steps led down the gray-painted passage to a thick steel door at the bottom. As the office door closed behind them Frank stopped, took a clip of ammunition from his pocket and slid it into the Thompson gun. At the snap of the breech Kurtz, halfway down the stairs, stopped in his tracks and stood, back stiffening. Frank moved down behind him and prodded him with the muzzle of the gun.

"What's my driver's name?" he said.

"Fairchild," the dispatcher told him.

"Does Mr. Fairchild have a wife, kids?"

"Yes. One child, a boy."

"You don't want that boy to grow up without a father, do you, Mr. Kurtz?"

The other man didn't answer.

"After we pull out of here, my colleague is going to drive you around for a while. Then he's going to turn you loose, free. You'll go home, and you'll find it's all just been a bad dream. Soon you and your family will have forgotten all about it, see?"

Frank kept his voice very soft but spoke distinctly, near the dispatcher's ear, so that the man could hear each word. "But if something should happen after the trucks pull out of here—if you should slip away from my friend, say—I want you to remember your family and Fairchild's family. You'll do that, won't you?" He jammed the gun with sudden force against Kurtz's spine and drove him, stumbling, down the stairs.

"Make it good!" he snarled as the dispatcher opened the door to the garage.

# CHAPTER THIRTEEN

T HE ARMORED TRUCK ROLLED along the empty streets on its heavy, hard-sprung chassis, jolting Frank and the driver uncomfortably about the cab. The hollow rumble of tires echoed in the tanklike body, a dull thunder that made conversation difficult. Frank was grateful at least for this, but the lumbering movement of the truck sent fresh waves of pain through his aching body till he wanted to groan aloud. Gripping the vertical metal bar that ran up the port-holed door next to him, he steadied himself as much as possible and waited for the ride to end.

He wondered if Ginther were having any trouble with the dispatcher. Everything had gone well enough at the O'Farrell office. There had been a few curious glances when Kurtz introduced him as a replacement for the "ailing" Olsen, but nothing out of the ordinary. The dispatcher had gone over their instructions once again, briefly, and a few minutes later they had been in the street, rolling through the mist-wet night. So much for that part of it, he thought, and wondered why he suddenly felt so strange. Then he understood—they had passed the point of no return.

He shrugged a little, and somehow it turned into a small shudder.

"Say, look," Frank said, turning to the driver, "when we get to the bank, would you mind standing outside guard and letting me stay in the truck? I hurt my back the other day, and standing in one place very long bothers it."

The driver nodded. "I don't mind," he said. Then, "How long you been with Van Ness?"

"Not long," Frank said. "How is this O'Farrell outfit to work for?"

"They're okay. A bunch of tough babies, though, everything by the book."

Ahead Frank could see the taillights of the front vehicle in their convoy. The other two trucks were close behind. They turned another corner—and were almost blinded by brilliant lights. The driver pulled to a stop.

As they sat, pinned under the powerful flood-lamps, a pair of plain-clothes cops came down the fine, peering into each cab. Frank felt himself go taut. As the cops reached them, Frank's driver opened a slit in his door and looked out.

"Put this one in the middle," the cop said to them, "about ten feet from the curb, facing straight into the street. Got it?"

"Yeah, got you," the driver said, and they were moving through, down to the front of the bank building. As his eyes recovered from the harsh glare of fights Frank began to look around. The street was an armed camp. All the vehicles on the side nearest the bank had been cleared away so that the curb was bare its full length. Across from the bank, about fifty feet in the direction from which they'd entered, were several police cars and motorcycles. The entire area was bathed in intense light from overhead, and at either end of the barricaded street floodlight trucks poured illumination over the entrances.

They pulled level with the bank, then swung in a short arc, out and away. Frank's driver maneuvered tail-first toward the curb. On either side of them the other trucks were positioning themselves similarly, angling in so that their back gates formed a semicircle facing the bank entrance. Engines were killed.

It was weirdly quiet around them once the motors were off, considering the area was daylight-bright. Only the sound of an occasional voice and the low throb of the generators for the searchlights penetrated the brilliant silence. After a while, the plain-clothes cops came up again and signaled.

"You'll have to cover from out here till I get the back end open," the driver told Frank, and they both got out. As Frank jumped down, pain hit him again—his battered body was beginning to stiffen from the cold and damp. He turned with the Thompson gun and watched as the driver went around to unlock the rear. After a moment the man stuck his head around one door and said, "Okay."

Gratefully, Frank got back into the truck.

The loading progressed behind him, heavy weights thumping onto the floor of the truck with regularity. The dim forms of blue-uniformed men were visible to him now across the street, stationed up and down its length. He knew that the darkened windows of the building above them concealed still more guns. There were four police cars in all and one unmarked black Ford sedan with searchlights on each side. He counted either six or seven motorcycles clustered together between the cars, radio sets crackling intermittently. He leaned back in the seat, trying to rest, knowing that he must conserve himself as much as possible.

A face appeared at the window, and there was a sharp rapping sound. Frank jolted up, hesitated a second, then slid open the peep-slot. "What is it?"

"I'm the supervisor, Burdette. I want to talk to you a minute, Nolan."

Now what? he thought, his brain working furiously. Cautiously, he opened the door, gun ready.

"Understand you're filling in for Olsen tonight." The man was slim, medium height, wearing a gray suit and soft felt hat. He had a snub-nosed revolver in the groin holster at his belt, the black handle protruding a little from one edge of his open coat.

"That's right."

"How come they didn't use one of the regular substitutes?"

"Don't know," Frank said. "This happened at the last minute, and it was pretty late—guess he couldn't get anybody else."

"You done this kind of work before?"

"Never anything just exactly like this," Frank said, hoping it was the right answer. The supervisor smiled.

"Well, neither have I, as a matter of fact," he said. "Just keep your eyes open, and don't be afraid to use that if you have to." He pointed to the short-muzzled Thompson.

"I won't," Frank promised. Burdette turned away, and Frank pulled the door closed again. After a moment he realized that he was sweating profusely in the cold, steel-smelling cab.

The clumping sounds stopped, and the bank lights went off suddenly. A moment later Fairchild climbed back inside and started the engine.

"Kee-rist!" the uniformed man swore, "these jokers are stop-watch happy. It'd be just too bad if a guy had to go to the can!" He slammed the truck into gear as the vehicle to their left pulled away and roared in behind it. The snap of the clutch hurled Frank against the back of the seat, and this time he could not repress a moan of pain.

"What's the matter, your back?" the driver asked.

Through clenched teeth, Frank said, "Don't worry about it—I'm all right."

They made a half-circle in the middle of the street, the other two trucks falling into position behind, and headed back down the way they had come in. As they passed the police vehicles six motorcycles streamed out to take up positions in front and behind them. They stopped a moment in the floodlight, and Frank saw the black sedan glide by, the supervisor in the front seat with another man. Then they were past, moving into comparative blackness, turning left toward the new Wellingford Trust Building. It was the route Frank had driven many times with Jim Fogherty.

A glance at his watch told him that they were perfectly on time as they started. He was not surprised—this operation was masterfully planned. He had braced the automatic gun, stock down, on the seat between his legs, the barrel nestling against his left shoulder and the breech-action turned away from the driver's line of vision. As they rode, he worked quietly with the small screwdriver, loosening the action till he could slide out the cartridge feeder-bar. This he dropped into one pocket, then tightened the screws again and put the small tool away. When he had finished, his watch read 2:03. They should be nearing the garage now.

The lead truck had opened up about a 50-foot gap, leaving one of the motorcycle escort riding along between the two of them. The cop was hunched uncomfortably, his black leather jacket shining wetly in their headlights, fur-lined collar turned up around his white crash-helmet. He weaved slowly from side to side to keep his balance while traveling at the caravan's tortuous 15-mile-an-hour pace. Further up Frank could make out the reddish-blue eyes of the two more policemen's cycles. He could not see the supervisor's sedan.

The fog had thickened, and lights were visible along the street for only about half a block. Tensely, he stared out into the pale mist, straining to catch a first glimpse of the all-night garage where Cat was supposed to be waiting.

He could not read the name of the next street on the sign-post, but his watch told him the garage was due to appear, right—*now!*

There was nothing but the mist.

Panic sprang up in him, an ugly, choking thing. Another street went by in the dark. *The garage must have closed—for some reason it must have shut down for the night!* What the hell would he do now? How could he get out? He would have to ride all the way to the other end with them, and by then Kurtz or Olsen would have sounded the alarm—and he'd be trapped!

And then he saw it.

At first it looked like another of the several stoplights they had passed, but then the red lettering blinked through the haze at him—KELLY'S NITE-OWL GARAGE. He almost sobbed in relief.

A fluid weakness washed through his veins, a slow trembling began in his stomach. He lowered his head, pressing the cold metal of the gun against his face. When he looked up they were passing under the sign—the garage entrance was a few feet farther on, in the middle of the block. He reached out and touched the guard's arm.

"Hey, look," Frank said, "isn't there somebody in the doorway over here?"

The driver leaned forward and looked past Frank. As he did the headlights appeared out of the darkness to their left, a huge, black automobile hurtled forward, swinging in a wide arc toward them. Frank saw the motorcycle cop up ahead veer suddenly away, slipping and going down on the wet pavement. *"Look out!"* Frank yelled and grabbed the wheel.

The black car came in fast under blinding headlights. Frank did not feel the impact, but suddenly he was lying sprawled against the door of the truck, his head pounding and a coolness on the side of his face. He reached up and felt his cheek where it was cut—not deeply. My God, he thought, he really laid into us—hope he didn't kill himself.

The driver, who had been thrown half underneath Frank, was struggling back to a sitting position, cursing steadily and fumbling for his pistol. "That crazy bastard, he cried.

Frank leaned forward and saw the running figures around them as the motorcycle escort rushed back to the accident.

"That guy ran right into us!" the driver said. "Keep ready—this could be trouble!" He pushed open the door on his side and dropped out to the street, crouching low. On the other side of the car Frank could see two officers dragging Cat from the crumpled sedan. Calm now, Frank reached across and twisted the steering wheel. It turned a few inches and stopped, grating metallically, the mechanism jammed solid. He picked up the two-way microphone and squeezed the trigger.

"Truck 0-116 to headquarters—come in, please."

He released the trigger, listened to the static crackle across his speaker and a voice saying, "Come in, 0-116." Frank pressed the handle again. "This is 0-116—we have had a minor accident—a collision—no trouble. Please send a wrecker to give us a tow the rest of the way in."

"Will you need additional escort?"

"No!" Frank answered. "We have plenty. Just send the tow truck." He switched off. Benson would be on his way already. It would take him four minutes exactly to reach them—though he knew it would seem both an instant and an eternity. The nearest contracted police tow-station was ten minutes off. That gave them exactly six minutes—360 seconds—to act.

Frank climbed down from the damaged truck, pressing a handkerchief to his cut cheek, and went over to where Cat was being questioned. Supervisor Burdette was shouldering his way through the group of cops as Frank came up.

"All right, break this up and get back to your positions, all of you but the sergeant—you're a perfect target standing around here. Come on, *move!*" The uniformed figures dispersed, leaving Cat in the grip of a large, beefy motorcycle cop. Burdette faced the small captive sternly. "What's going on here, mister?"

Even Frank was amazed at the transformation. The person he saw was nothing like the one he knew as Cat. This man was shrunken and terrified, a whining little Milquetoast. He was dressed in a baggy tweed suit, crushed felt hat a half-size too big for him and a garish hand-painted tie. He was a picture of comic tragedy, crying with chagrin and horror at what he had done. The tears that streaked his little face were real.

"Came barreling out of that garage and ran right into the boys here," the cop said gruffly. "Says he was late for home and wasn't looking where he was going."

The O'Farrell Company supervisor walked over toward the garage entrance, turned and studied the car tracks leading out across the damp pavement. Slowly he returned to where the others were standing beside the wreck.

"Came out pretty fast, didn't you, mister?"

Cat sobbed afresh. "I—I didn't realize how—how late, and I knew that Ethel—that she would—" His small shoulders shook pitifully as he buried his head in his hands. "And now, when she sees the car—" he moaned weakly.

"Well, you've made a nice mess of things," Burdette mumbled, looking at the wrecked front end of the armored car. Frank stepped forward.

"Sir," he said, "I've called for a tow-truck. They could pull us on down to the bank—we wouldn't have to transfer the money here in the street."

Burdette looked at him in surprise, noticing the blood on Frank's face. "Won't work at all, eh?" he said, indicating the truck.

"No, sir. I tried to turn the wheel a few minutes ago, and it was jammed. So I called the wrecker—it should be here any minute."

The supervisor nodded thoughtfully. He did not seem quite satisfied. But he said, "That was quick thinking, Nolan." He turned to the policeman again. "This is a bad business," he said. "We're sitting ducks here, and I don't like it. I think we'd better keep a few of the men here and get the rest of this outfit off the street."

"Yes, sir," the motorcycleman said.

"Leave a third of the escort and have the rest of them take the other trucks in."

The motorcyclist nodded and started back to give the necessary orders.

"Is everyone in your truck all right?" Burdette asked Frank.

"Yes, sir."

"All right, I want you men to loosen up your guns and stay ready. This may be on the level, but you can't tell—it may be something fancy. I'll be coming with you." He looked around at

Cat. "I think you'd better stick with me, mister. I want to talk to you some more."

The little man nodded miserably and sat down on the running board of his demolished Packard.

Frank and Fairchild, the driver, returned to the crippled armored car. A feeling of exaltation raced through Shelby—Burdette was playing their game as well as he could possibly have hoped. He had been certain the supervisor would not want to keep the entire convoy exposed for the sake of one truck. Still, he might have chosen to have them all wait—and if he had it would have meant some shooting and a dangerous, long-odds race through the city. This way their job was far easier—now if only Arnie would hurry they would be all right. He glanced back down the street—and stopped. He stared, horror-stricken, at the sight that met his eyes.

Coming toward them, lights flashing, were not one—but *two* tow-trucks!

# CHAPTER FOURTEEN

T
HE TRUCK BENSON WAS DRIVING reached the scene of the
accident first, the other wrecker only a short distance behind.
Frank was relieved to see that Arnie had not lost his nerve. Boldly,
the big man pulled up in front of the crippled armored car and
backed into position. The second truck stopped alongside him
and the driver leaned out, frowning. Frank hurried over.

"Hey," the driver said, calling to Benson. "What are you
doing there? This is my call."

Ignoring him, Benson walked around to the back of his
truck and began lowering the lift chain. Frank approached the
other tow-truck.

"Looks like we got a little crossed up here," he said
smoothly, looking around to see if Burdette were coming. "I'll
tell you what—that old Packard there has got to be moved too.
Goes all the way down to Brooklyn. You can have the job if you
want it."

The driver looked dubious. He glanced at Benson, who was
just finishing hooking up to the armored truck. From the corner
of his eye Frank saw the supervisor walking toward them.

"It's a better fee," Frank said.

"Well—"

"What's the trouble now?" Burdette said, coming up at a
brisk walk.

"Looks like somebody doubled up on the call," Frank said.
"I told this guy he could probably take the Packard if he wanted
to."

The supervisor looked annoyed. "If you don't mind, Nolan, I'm still in charge here. Get back to your truck." He turned to the driver. "Let's get moving, we're wasting too damn much time."

Frank had walked out of earshot now. As he passed the old car where Cat was sitting, head in hands, he said, "Give them an address in Brooklyn." Cat nodded without looking up, and Frank went on to the armored car. A moment later he saw the driver of the second tow-truck come over and say something to the little man. Cat stood up to talk to him.

Fairchild was not in the cab, and Frank rapped sharply on the window leading to the back of the truck. The guard's face appeared after a moment.

"We going to go?" the man asked.

"Any minute now. Listen," Frank said, "I don't like the look of things. I think you'd better take this in case we run into trouble. You're in a better position to use it than I am." Without waiting for an answer, he shoved the Thompson gun back through the small window.

The guard seemed about to protest, then said, "Hey, thanks!" taking the more powerful weapon.

"Let me have your rifle," Frank said. Just as the gun was being passed through to him, a clattering noise began from up front, and the nose of the truck rose a few feet in the air. Fairchild piled in through the door on the driver's side and said, "That did it— here we go." Frank pushed the rifle down beside him out of sight.

He heard the motorcycle engines fire up and strained to see out over the hood. Burdette came along on the other side and said, "You men stay on the ready. This looks on the level, but you can never tell. We've got a couple of the cycle boys with us, and I'm riding up front in the tow-truck. Just in case this might be something fancy, I'm taking the little guy in the Packard with us. He'll have a good seat if he has any buddies around planning to start something." He glanced back to where Cat was standing and chuckled. "Not likely, though," he said and went back toward the front. Fairchild grinned after him. "See what I mean about these guys?" He counted: "Three, four, five, *six* guards with guns, radio, a chopper, and the boss himself riding along—all because some little jerk bumps into one of their trucks. These characters don't take chances."

Frank nodded, sitting back in the seat. He hadn't counted on Burdette's coming with them. That complicated things. On the other hand, Cat would be with them, which he hadn't considered, and that might balance it out. They'd know soon, anyway. So far, they were still in business.

Frank's watch read 2:17 A.M. Twelve minutes had passed since the accident—it seemed a lot longer. If nothing stopped them they would reach the turn-off in two more minutes. He had to get the rest of this over with quickly.

Frank looked over at the driver. As they passed near another streetlight he saw that Fairchild's holster was still unbuttoned. He reached across with a smooth motion and lifted the gun from its case.

"Hey," the other said, surprised. "What are you doing?"

"Shut up," Frank told him. He raised the gun, pulling back the hammer with an ominous snap. "Keep steady or you'll never live to find out. This is a holdup. I'll kill you if you move an inch."

Another streetlamp illuminated the inside of the cab, and he saw the shock and terror in Fairchild's face.

"You—you're nuts," the man stammered. "You'll never make it."

"If we don't you won't either," Frank promised him. "So just sit still until you're told what to do." He reached across and ripped the microphone from the dash, tossing the disconnected head to the floor.

"Now you listen to me, mister, if you want to stay alive," Frank growled. "We're going to stop in a few seconds. You open your peep and I'll fill it with a piece of lead. When we stop I'll tell you to get out. Do it fast, then lie down on the ground and stay there, no matter what happens. Stay till I tell you what to do next." He thrust the point of the gun into the driver's ribs and felt the man wince away in fear and pain. "Get that?"

"Yes, I'll do it!"

"Fine—now take it real easy."

They were slowing down, nearing the turn-off. By now the others should have Burdette under control-only the cops would remain to be taken care of. The truck suddenly pulled into the curb and stopped.

*"Hold it!"* Frank gritted. He heard the roar of the motor-cycles, caught sight of one as it swung wide, circling back to see what was wrong.

Frank jabbed with the pistol. "Out!" he commanded, *"get out!"* The driver threw open the door and dropped down, Frank quick behind him. "Okay, don't move," he whispered.

The first policeman was walking toward Benson, removing his gloves. He had one of them halfway off when the big man took a step forward, drew something from his belt and swung it in a short, hard arc to the uniformed man's head. The man crumpled.

On the other side of the wrecker Cat was pointing a gun at the second cop. Frank waved his own weapon. "Don't make a move, blue boy, or you get it from this side, too." Cat stepped forward and pulled the half-drawn revolver from the startled policeman's hand.

"All right now," Frank said, turning to the driver. "Get around back." At the rear of the truck Frank made a motion with his gun. "Open it." The driver obeyed. "Now get in."

"What's going on?" the guard inside demanded.

"Nothing you'll be able to do anything about," Frank told him. "That gun I gave you doesn't work." He slammed the door in the startled face and locked it, dropping the key in his pocket. He went around front again.

They had stopped by a short, narrow alley near their turn-off. He ran across, grabbed one of the motorcycles and wheeled it over to the entrance. Benson and Cat were just finishing tying and gagging the two policemen as he came by.

"Arnie, get that other bike," he said. "Cat, help me transfer Burdette to the truck."

Moving hurriedly, they went out to the street again. It was still deserted.

"How much time have we got?" Cat panted.

"I don't know. Burdette radioed ahead that we were waiting for the tow-car. They don't know for sure how long that'll take, but they'll probably give us ten minutes. Maybe more."

"Maybe less," Cat said.

The supervisor was sitting calmly in the front of the wrecker, his wrists handcuffed to the steering wheel. Cat freed him and, with a gun to the slender man's spine, marched him around back of the armored vehicle.

"Inside," Frank said, opening the door again.

Burdette hesitated. "You're kidding yourselves," he said. "You can't get out of the city—you haven't a chance." Cat shoved viciously, sending the supervisor sprawling through the door.

"Let's move!" Frank sprinted for the front of the truck. Cat hurried to join Arnie in the wrecker, and a moment later they were in motion, Benson sending them screeching around the comer and away from the Wellingford Bank.

The incredible had happened—they'd made it!

Frank fought to hold on inside the careening cab, grabbing for purchase. At last, jammed into one comer behind the steering wheel, he managed to stop being thrown about like a sack of seed. The cut on his face was bleeding again, and he stopped it with his sleeve, his other arm wrapped around the steering post.

In less than four minutes they would be at the rendezvous. Now was the time to put the final portion of his plan—the part he had not told Hanford about—into action. Reaching up, he pounded hard on the rear window. After a moment a hand appeared in the open slot, then a face. It was Burdette.

"What do you want?" the supervisor said.

"I just thought you guys might like to have your guns back," he said.

The sound of the tires changed abruptly, and he knew they were traveling over dirt instead of pavement now, winding down to the shallow depression containing the big shed. They came almost to a stop, turned sharply and pulled into blackness. A moment later he heard the doors swing shut, and then the lights came on.

Frank opened his door and stepped down to the bare floor of the shed. The big auto-carrier was parked along one wall, its high cab facing the door, the long rails on which the armored car would ride reaching almost the length of the building. The two had not yet been joined—the rear ramp of the trailer was down, ready to receive its burden. Under the hood of the cab, he knew, was the other of the two high-powered engines. Special shock-absorbers and anti-sway bars made the rig capable of speeds over a hundred, loaded. With it, they could enter the New Jersey Turnpike within the next few minutes, the captured armored car shrouded on the trailer, and be hundreds of miles away before daylight. After leaving the other end of the freeway—showing a forged time-card with a different time of entry—no one could possibly suspect the missing money truck was being leisurely looted three states away. It was the final stage in Frank Shelby's greatest achievement.

He grinned wryly. It was the only one that wasn't going to come off.

Ginther came up on the run. "You made it!" he yelled.

"How's Kurtz?" Frank said.

"I dropped him off on the edge of town, like you said."

"How is he?"

"I tapped him on the head." Ginther shrugged. "He'll be okay. He turned and walked over to the tow-truck where Benson was climbing down. "We did it, huh?" Big Arnie grinned at him.

Cat was standing near the cab, blinking in the unexpectedly bright room, looking up to where Joe Hines stood on the side of the carrier.

"Hey, pal," Hines was saying, "did I ever get the soft touch— you should have seen this babe I had to watch!"

Slowly, Frank began to be aware that something was wrong around him—something that did not jibe with what his brain told him should be. He straightened up and looked around again. Gradually, realization penetrated the haze of weariness in his mind—he whirled and ran to Ginther, grabbing the younger man by the arm.

"Where's Hanford?" he demanded.

Ginther was frowning. "Hell, I don't know. The truck was here when I came in. I figured he'd been already and gone. Why?"

Frank felt the sweat beginning to coat his face. "Who was here when you came in?"

Ginther moved his head. "Just Joe," he said.

Frank ran across to where Hines and Cat were talking. "Did you see Hanford?" he cried. "When you came in, I mean?"

The slender man jumped down, shaking his head. "The place was empty."

He grabbed Hines by both arms, shaking him furiously. "What are you trying to pull!" he yelled. "You sonofabitch, what are you trying—"

Hines twisted away from his grip, his face showing anger and pain. Frank stumbled, his legs refusing to respond to the shift in balance, and he fell against the side of the carrier.

"Hey!" Hines said. "What's the matter with you?"

Frank sagged weakly, clawing for a grip on the truck and gasping for breath. Get hold of yourself, Shelby! You know where he is, and you know why he's gone there. Get up! Make yourself stand up—there's not much time left!

The others were staring at him as he raised his head. "All right, let's break this up," his voice rasped hoarsely. "The cops will have the whole island locked up tight in about ten more minutes. If we aren't on the other side and heading down the Turnpike by then, we'll never be." He waved toward the armored car. "Get it on here—let's go!"

His words galvanized the others. The chain pulley they'd rigged was pulled around and the task of transferring the heavy truck was begun. Frank pushed himself up and began walking around to the far side of the wrecker. He found he could barely lift his legs. His arms were like lead weights strapped to his body.

The chain-hoist lifted the front end of the armored car clear of the tow-truck and began dragging it toward the carrier. Frank stood next to the steel-sided machine, touching it with one hand as though guiding its progress, until it inched its way past him. Then he stepped behind it, out of sight of the men working the pulleys.

His hand, with the key in it, raised to the door. Sweat dropped down beneath his arms and over his chest. He struggled with his shaking hands. Only a few seconds remained. With a desperate stab, the key struck the slot, hung, and slipped into position.

Benson's head popped around the end of the truck. "Watch out!" the big man yelled, "she's going up!" And he was gone again.

Frank gripped the bars of the rear window, resting his head against the steel as the truck pulled him slowly along. He realized that tears were running down his face. With one hand he reached down and twisted the key—the handle turned. He released it and faced around, half staggering, half running to the parked tow-truck. At the truck's tailgate, he paused and lifted a loose length of chain back into the bed, then dragged himself on to the door on the driver's side.

He did not look back when he heard the first surprised cry, followed by a crash of gunfire.

The controls of the tow-truck were not familiar to him. He searched for the starter, found it, twisted the key and felt the engine kick—and stall. The truck was still in gear. Glancing back, he saw uniformed guards crouching on the dirt floor at either side of the uptilted armored car, firing at the men around the carrier. The staccato burst of the Thompson gun filled the room with ear-splitting noise, and Frank saw Hines, standing behind the cab, spin backward and fall under the wheels of the big transporter.

Frank held down the clutch and turned the starter again. The powerful Chrysler engine turned slowly, failing to take hold—his false start had flooded it. With deadly calm, Frank depressed the accelerator slowly, turned the starter again. Behind him, the back window suddenly shattered, splintering glass down around his neck and shoulders.

The engine fired.

He got it into gear, raking the cogs unmercifully. The wheels spun as he threw out the clutch, and the truck began to move. In front of him the doors of the shed loomed solidly, thick beams jutting out like wooden sinews. The Thompson gun was roaring again, and he was aware of a pattering thud against the metal of the cab. They were trying for him in earnest. And then he hit the door.

He exploded through with a grinding shriek of wood against metal, and then he was outside. He swerved dangerously before getting his bearings, jerked the wheel around and headed for the highway. The bullets were no longer after him—he could not hear the sound of firing over the engine's noise. He located the headlight switch just as he reached the paved roadway and felt a surge of relief when one of the two front lamps, unbroken by the collision with the door, came on.

A desperate excitement was in him now, unleashing reserves of strength he had not known he possessed. Ahead was the Club

Xanadu and Nancy—Hanford would be there by now, too. He would need all the power in the hopped-up truck to get there in time.

He slowed for the toll station at the bridge, handing out his coin. As he did so, he glanced in his rear vision mirror, and froze at what he saw. Coming up fast, braking for the toll gate, was the cab section from the carrier.

As Frank swung out onto the highway, he saw the machine slide to a halt at the toll gate, caught a glimpse of blond hair, then heard the roar of the powerful engine. It was Ginther, driving the cab of the other truck. Ahead of them were twenty miles of highway.

Frank's foot smashed down hard on the accelerator. His engine responded with a forward surge. He watched the speedometer needle swing upward across the black dial, reaching for 60, 70, 80. The machine began to tremble slightly, tires absorbing thousands of tiny imperfections from the pavement with a hard humming sound; vision beginning to blur out of the corner of his eyes as the headlights danced a hot pool ahead on the featureless asphalt.

He looked through the rear mirror. The lights were there, behind him—Ginther was gaining. The cab section of the autocarrier was lighter than Frank's tow-truck, and on the straight road it had more speed. As though to gain the last fraction of an inch of accelerator travel, Frank forced the pedal against the floor until his leg ached. The needle was rising slowly, now, sliding past 90, toward 100, hanging, hesitantly, then inching gradually past.

The lights were less than a quarter-mile behind him. Ahead, he knew, the taut-stretched ribbon of highway ended, and several miles of winding road through the low foothills began. If he could reach them he might be able to hold his own. Watching fascinated, he saw the headlights creeping closer—a hundred yards—fifty. His speedometer was frozen at 110 miles per hour, the en-gine-wail a piercing monster's cry. The truck was too low-geared for more speed. Now he only prayed the straining power-plant would hold together.

And then they hit the first curve.

Frank saw it coming, stabbed the brakes and swung the wheel to the right. He had slowed too soon, though, and the other truck moved up till they were bumper to bumper. Just before they entered the turn Frank felt a sudden shock—Ginther had hit him. He fought for control, holding the careening truck on the road with desperate effort. He made it through, then noticed that Ginther had fallen back slightly. On the next curve he gained yet a little more.

The tow-truck was faster in the turns. Frank was sure of that now. Probably because there was no weight over the rear wheels on Ginther's machine. For the next mile he widened the gap steadily. As long as they came on one turn after another he was all right, but on each short, straight length of road he lost his advantage rapidly. And he remembered that the road had no turns for the last five miles before reaching the club. If Ginther stayed as close as he was now he would catch up then. Frank had to make up more time in the corners. Gradually, he began pushing his truck deeper and deeper before braking.

A sharp left loomed up in the headlights. He held the accelerator down until the sweat began to spring out on his face. Then he pounded the brake pedal down and threw the big truck in, feeling the tires slip against the pavement, holding it in a half-slide through the sharpest angle, then letting the truck straighten out again under power. He tried it again on the next curve, and the next. Slowly but steadily he pulled away.

There was not yet enough margin, though—he couldn't relax yet. Turn by turn, he had to press on. The next was another left-hander. Dimming his lights, checking for the approach of cars from the other direction, he cut deeply down across the oncoming lane, allowing the speed of the truck to carry him through the bend, then hitting the gas hard, wavering back across the road to his own side, slipping to the very edge of the pavement before straightening out. His mouth was dry as he looked down into the inky darkness waiting beyond the shoulder—a straight drop, how many feet he did not know.

Then, just as he thought he might be going to make it after all, they were out of the winding section. The lights behind him began to gain. Inexorably they moved up. If only he had kept one of the guns, if only he could stop and fight! But he couldn't—he was at Ginther's mercy. The other man could get close enough to begin shooting at Frank or his tires or he could wait till they reached the club and be more certain of his aim. Or Ginther could try to run him off the road, though that might kill them both. It would be nice to take Ginther with him—but it wouldn't help Nancy with Hanford. If only he hadn't been such a fool, Frank raged to himself.

Something ahead flickered in his eyes.

By the time he had seen the turn and recognized it it was almost too late. The final right-hand curve that straightened the road out into the five-mile run to Club Xanadu. He had forgotten about it entirely. Lined with trees to the right, it was protected by a low guardrail on the left. Unlike the corners through the foothills, this one was not banked but swerved flatly in a 45 degree angle to the north. With panic in his throat Frank put on the brakes, hitting them too hard and locking them. He felt the truck begin to slide, eased the pressure, then stamped down again. He gripped the wheel in fingered vices, holding it in a straight line pointed right at the empty verge. His will fought him, telling him to try to turn, but his mind knew that to move the wheel yet meant disaster. He braced rigidly against the back of the seat, braking, braking, watching the white fence sweep up. The speedometer whirled down from 80 to 70 to 60—still too fast—he was into the corner, he was speeding across the highway, over the center line, plunging toward the rail and the sharp drop of the bank. At the final instant he turned the wheel.

The tires began their low-voiced scream, straining against the roadway as the coarse, black surface tried to pry them from the rims. Sparks showered from the metal edges as the rubber rolled down and under, beneath tons of weight. Frank felt the truck lurch drunkenly, swaying on the edge of a spin, threatening to release its awesome kinetic energy in a sudden, violent series of hurtling flips and rolls. He held the steering wheel against the sickening release of the rear tires, felt the tail begin to swing around, and then the front tires losing traction. He had turned the truck, but it was coming around too fast, sliding, shearing down the distance of paved road between it and the side, beginning to finger the dirt shoulder into spurts of dust and gravel.

And then the slide took over, seizing control from him and turning the wheel to a useless thing in his hands. As he steeled himself for the first wrenching gyration there was a tremendous impact—the tail struck the guardrail a solid, shuddering blow. As though a giant hand had reached out and touched the truck it was magically headed in the right direction again, the highway stretching out at a proper angle. The tires were biting into pavement, pulling him forward.

He was through the turn.

Frank looked into his rear view mirror. Behind him the other truck was traveling in a slow series of moving pictures that would remain in his mind forever. Less maneuverable than his own machine, Ginther's had no chance. Intent until the last instant on overtaking, the blond gunman had braked even later than he. So far as Frank could see Ginther did not attempt the turn at all.

His first reaction was one of amazement, a dazed wondering at what the other vehicle was doing—why it was no longer following him—why it was rising weirdly off the ground. As he stared the truck left the highway, penetrating the guardrail like a projectile, its headlight beams searching the nothingness of the night. Very slowly, as it fell, the truck began to turn on its back, then dropped below Frank's sight. The dust from the roadside lifted in a gray-brown pall, marking the spot where the cab had gone over. An instant later there was a dull crash, and the cloud grew bright with orange light. A billowing flash rose into the air, blackening at its roiling edges as it lifted, then turned coal-red from the intensity of the flames below. Frank could not see the truck or the spot where Ginther had fallen. For a moment he slowed, touching his brakes, then moved his foot gently onto the accelerator again.

There was no need to stop.

# CHAPTER FIFTEEN

THE DARK SHAPE OF CLUB XANADU loomed out of the night so suddenly that the speeding truck almost shot past it. With shrilling brakes, the big machine lost momentum and swerved off the highway, careering across the deserted parking lot until it came to a slamming stop against the curb in front of the building. Frank Shelby threw open the door and jumped down. His legs buckled an instant, then held—he cursed under his breath and started up the steps to the front door.

It was unlocked, and he pushed his way into the darkened lobby. The emptiness of the place was disturbing. Always before, at night, he had seen the foyer crowded with well-dressed, noisy men and women, and now the hollow silence seemed eerie and somehow threatening. Shrugging off an uneasy tremor, he turned and hurried up the carpeted stairs.

Nancy's room was empty. He glanced inside briefly, then continued quietly down the hall. A slab of light issued from under the door of his own apartment, spreading yellowly across the carpet. Voices came from inside, a man's and a woman's. He wished he had kept one of the guards' guns—but he hadn't. His only weapon was surprise. Setting himself, Frank took a deep breath and lunged at the door.

As his shoulder struck wood, everything seemed to happen at once, a blur of impressions that numbed his brain. First, the jolting pain of contact, a splintering sound as the punished boards bent inward, then a quick release and helpless plunging as the door swung freely open and sent him sprawling, off balance, to the floor.

A woman screamed.

Slowly, pulling himself to his hands and knees, he realized that the door had not been locked; it had yielded too easily under the force of his attack. When he looked up, he was staring into the leveled muzzle of Stanley Hanford's automatic.

"Get up," the old man said, and his voice was harsh and charged with danger. Nancy was sitting in a straight wooden chair, her arms tied behind her. Vikki was not present. Instantly Frank knew that Hanford had learned what had happened.

"So you came after me anyway," Hanford said. "Good! A lesser man, seeing that his enemy had escaped the trap, might have fled. But not Frank Shelby, eh?"

"You haven't escaped, Hanford," Frank said flatly. "They'll be here looking for you as soon as they find out it's your hoods they've just picked off. It'll be all over soon; now it's just a question of whether you're smart enough to let it go at attempted robbery or whether you want to do something dumb and have murder added to the rap."

Hanford laughed unpleasantly. "Don't be stupid, Frank. The boys won't talk—they're far too wise. If they weren't they wouldn't be working for me. No, we won't be disturbed. And that's fortunate." He smiled. "For it so happens murder is *precisely* what I plan—you are going to pay the way Willie Dolan did, or do you remember?"

Frank remembered. The look of fanaticism in the old man's eyes was the same he'd seen there five years before—the night they'd picked Willie up. The eyes had burned white-hot, then. Forced to watch the things Hanford did, Frank had become ill. At first he'd been ashamed of himself for his weakness but later that had changed—he had recovered and had even helped pack the thing that had been a man into the 100-gallon drum of lime and roll it into 35 feet of water—had helped because he thought that nobody should ever have to look at Willie again, the way he was, and because Frank's capacity for horror was suddenly gone, replaced by a cold realization of the thing he'd become part of. And that night he had left. He'd put the old man, and all he stood for, behind and sworn never to let himself look on that face again. Now, having no choice, he looked—and saw the thing he dreaded most.

"Look, Hanford," he said, "you may have a score to even with me, but that doesn't concern Nancy. Let her go. Don't take a chance you don't have to—she doesn't know anything, and she can't hurt you. Turn her loose now."

The old man smiled. "Very good!" he said. "Please go on, I'm listening."

Frank flushed at the mocking tone of Hanford's voice. It was useless, he knew—worse than useless, because it was exactly what the other wanted from him—a plea for mercy.

Hanford saw the look of understanding in Frank's face and nodded. "Yes," he said, "it's true. I would not let your wife go even if she were not a danger to me—and we both know she is—because that is to be part of your penalty."

The little man began moving back from him, past where Nancy was sitting, kneeling down as he reached the huge aquarium at the far end of the room. "In fact," he said, "we will *start* with your charming wife."

Hanford slid back a panel in the base of the large fixture, reached in and began to turn a valve with one hand. Frank heard the rush and gurgle of water after a moment and saw the level behind the glass plunge rapidly downward.

Desperately, he searched the room with his eyes, seeking some weapon or means of offense. Whatever it was Hanford was up to, only force could stop him now. Suddenly, his glance fell on the thing he was looking for—the knife-case, hanging from the wall nearest him. A spark of hope flared—and then died.

In the center of the case two hooks stood empty, the absence of dust between them betraying a recent presence.

"Looking for this by any chance?"

Frank swung his gaze back and saw the dull gleam of metal in the old man's hand, eight inches of wickedly curved steel extending from a slender, unguarded handle. It was a throwing knife, glass sharp and perfectly balanced. He remembered that Hanford knew how to use it, too.

Having finished what he was doing with the big tank the old man closed the panel again and stood up, shifting the knife to his right hand and taking the gun in his left. He moved slowly toward Nancy.

"A fine instrument," he said, motioning with the knife. "Made by Polynesians, and beautifully crafted. It's commonly thought the Islanders did not know how to work metal until the white man came, but anthropologists now claim they passed through an iron age a good while prior to that. In any case, they seem to have gained a considerable skill in the meantime, because this is among the best of my collection."

The hypnotically smooth voice did not deceive Frank, and as Hanford moved closer to his wife he prepared for a final try. He measured the distance between them, calculating the number of steps it would take him to reach the old man—get his hands around that scrawny neck....

He took a half step forward.

"Stand where you are!" Hanford cried, "or I'll cut her throat open!" The knife had moved as swiftly as a krait—it pressed against the skin of Nancy's neck, making a thin, white line across the constricting flesh.

Frank held himself motionless, body rigid.

The old man's breathing came quickly. "If you force me this will be sudden and final. Don't move like that again. There is no need in any case, since I don't intend to hurt Mrs. Shelby at all." He turned and put the tip of the blade under the shoulder of Nancy's sleeveless cotton dress and split the fabric outward. He did the same to the other side, then bent and slashed the light material all the way to the girl's hip, working his knife very carefully.

"What the hell are you doing?" Frank demanded.

The old man straightened up, grinning. "Why, I thought it might be pleasant for your wife to take a nice, cooling dip in our pool downstairs." He sliced the ropes then, pulling Nancy to her feet and twisting one arm behind her back before she could move. The ripped dress fell down—her slender, tanned body trembled nakedly, clothed only in white panties and brassiere.

Frank looked in amazement at his wife and at Hanford, then at the last dregs of greenish water draining from the aquarium tank, "A swim—" he said. And then he understood.

"You're insane!" he cried. "You're completely out of your mind!"

The little man broke into a delighted laugh. "So!" he chuckled, "you understand already, do you? Yes, your wife will swim with my little friends, the piranhas—they are waiting for her even now. But don't think I am being unfair. It is a test—I have decided to give you both a chance, you see. If she can swim the length of the pool and survive, then the two of you are free!"

It was a lie. Even through the haze of fear and anger Frank had enough sense to know it was a lie. Hanford way toying, now—enjoying himself hugely. Suddenly, though, this gave Frank an idea. The old man wanted to savor their final minutes—wanted it with a deep, psychological need. Wanted it so badly, perhaps, that he would be eager to think Frank was fooled.

He allowed a look of hope to come into his eyes. "She hasn't got a chance, though," he argued.

"Of course she has—in fact it is her *only* chance." Hanford smiled.

Frank appeared to consider. He looked at Nancy. "Can you try, darling?" he asked. "Can you do it?"

She shuddered, once, looking helplessly back at him. "I—yes, I—I'll try," she said.

"Good!" Hanford said, loosening his grip on the girl's arm. "It will be necessary for us all to go downstairs, then."

Frank waited, ready now, watching for Nancy to move just a foot or two out of the way. She took a tentative step forward and stopped. He had not counted on what happened next. As he prepared to throw himself forward, Nancy suddenly turned and slashed at the old man's wrist. Hanford cried out in pain as the gun spun out of his hand. Frank charged, then, seeing the knife come up, aimed to dart into his body, knowing he could not evade it and not caring, if only he could reach Hanford....

A voice cried "Stop!"

The sound of it froze him. Hanford too whirled around, involuntarily. Vikki was standing in the doorway leading to her rooms, looking at them. She wore a pair of black, close-fitting pants and a white halter which exposed her lightly-muscled midriff and the deep cleft of her breasts. A small, blue-barreled revolver was in her hand, and it was pointed straight at Frank. All hope went out of him as the girl came on into the room, and he let himself sag weakly against the side of the couch.

"Excellent, Vikki!" the old man cried, grinning widely. "Your sense of timing is still superb!" He moved forward, toward the place where his gun had fallen previously.

"And now *you* stop," the dark-haired girl said evenly. Hanford looked up in amazement, not certain that she was talking to him. He saw she was.

"Vikki, what is the meaning of this?" he said, taking another hesitant step toward the gun.

"If you move again I'll kill you."

Something in her tone convinced him. His mouth opened slightly, but no words came out. He stepped backward, eyes fixed on the barrel of her gun.

"Don't do this," he finally succeeded in whispering. "Don't let him make a fool of you—he tried to destroy us, don't you understand? He's killed the others and tricked you!"

"I know everything; that's happened," she said. "I've listened from the hall."

"Don't you see then? He's betrayed us—he's a murderer!"

Vikki laughed—a short, harsh sound. "That's amusing, Stanley, coming from you," she said. "I think Frank was right, you know—you really are mad. You should be treated as a raving animal would."

The old man's voice shook as he spoke. "What are you going to do?" he said, shrinking from the menace of the gun.

"To begin with, I'm going to let Frank and his wife go."

"*You fool!* You don't know what you're doing!"

"Strange," she said, "but I think I do. I really think I do—for the first time in so many years. All of this time I haven't known, I've stayed here and pretended that you really weren't the way I knew you were."

Her voice was low, almost dreamlike as she talked now, and Frank had the thought that she was speaking for him, even though her eyes never left Hanford for a moment.

"At first, of course, I told myself I was waiting for Frank, that I'd only stay until he came again. Then I stopped believing in his return, but still I stayed. This was the only life I knew, so why should I leave it? I told myself that I wasn't really a part of the things that were going on—that it was no concern of mine. But it was, of course. I know now that it was."

For the first time her eyes flickered toward Frank, then back again. "When you did come back, I made him promise not to harm you and to let you stay after the robbery. I thought you'd be forced to stay anyway. I even warned him of your escape—yes, I did that. I didn't want you to leave, don't you see, Frank? But I didn't know they were going to kill Jim—you must believe that, I didn't know."

"I believe you," Frank said quietly.

"I was such a fool. Afterward I knew in my heart that he had lied to me and that he wouldn't keep his promise even about you. But I was so used to making myself believe what I wanted to that I couldn't stop—even then. I still thought everything would be all right, after the job was over. If only your wife weren't here, I thought! So tonight I didn't wait for either of you to call. An hour after you'd gone I unlocked her and told her she could go. I called the taxi and had it waiting. Then I gave her her things and told her to go away.

Vikki smiled, with unexpected sadness in her face. "But she wouldn't," she said softly. "She wouldn't go. I told her what would happen to her, but she insisted on staying, and then Stanley came back and found us ... "

The little man could not restrain himself. "Don't you understand? She *knew!* It was a plot between them, and she was waiting for him to return after his vile treachery."

Vikki shook her head. "No," she said, "I only thought she meant to stay and fight for him, that she didn't understand what had happened. It was later on, when you got the report on the radio, that I saw that she had known all along. And it was then I decided to do this, Stanley."

She turned to Frank, her eyes searching his face for understanding. "I realized that Nancy must have known how small your chances were, and yet she was willing to risk being caught again—killed if you failed—because she loved you so much. And I knew all at once how wrong I had been. I wanted you to love me, Frank, but suddenly I realized that I didn't have that right."

Frank wanted to reach out to her and tell her that it was all right, that he forgave her for everything and that, in fact, there was nothing to forgive. But she seemed to see this in his eyes, for she smiled abruptly and gladly at him.

"That's when I decided that I would do at least one decent thing—for both of you."

He sensed it before he saw it—a slight shifting of the old man's body from across the room. Frank looked over quickly and saw the small hand dip back, come quickly forward.

"*Vikki!*" he yelled and jumped toward her. But he was too late. Bright steel winked in the room. The girl gasped and clutched at her stomach, then slowly began to crumple to the floor. Frank saw Hanford stooping over for his fallen gun, and he dived down to pull Vikki's revolver from her hand. As he whirled around the room erupted with sound. A giant, red-hot hand gripped his shoulder and spun him to the floor.

Frank raised himself up and squeezed off a shot at the dodging figure of the little man. Then, dizzy from shock, he scrambled to his knees, seeing Hanford already at the door. His shoulder was numb, but there was no pain yet, and he rested his hand on the end of the couch to aim. Hanford fired again. Frank pulled his hand down, and the aquarium tank behind him shattered, pouring glass shards out onto the floor. He heard the door slam as Hanford went out.

Vikki sat hunched over beside him. One hand was closed tightly around the hilt of the knife where it protruded from the patch of smooth flesh beneath her breasts. As he reached over, the knife came away in her taloned fingers—he saw the blue-lipped mouth in her belly begin to ooze thick blood.

Her eyes, clouded with pain and shock, were fastened to his face, and he saw the pleading there. "Forgive me," she whispered. "Oh, please, darling—forgive me."

"Don't talk, Vikki, it's all right. It's all right." But he saw that she did not hear him.

"Nancy—loves you," the girl murmured, "even more-more than I could. She's—very good, Frank—" She looked up, suddenly, and for an instant her eyes were clear.

"Good-by—darling," she said.

He put his arms around the girl and tried to lift her, but his left hand fell uselessly to his side. He stood and turned to Nancy.

"See if you can help her," he said. "Try to get her onto the couch—
I've got to go." He turned and went toward the door and out of
the room.

As he came through the door, crouched low, finger tight on
the trigger of Vikki's gun, Hanford was starting down the stairs.
Frank ducked, and the woodwork by his head split open, show-
ering his face with splinters. The sound of the shot echoed and
died. He was up and moving again.

Hanford was almost at the bottom of the stairs. Frank shot
without aiming and missed. Vikki's gun was a short-barreled .22
caliber—he would have to get close if he hoped to do any good
with it. He had fired twice. Four shots left. He saw Hanford hesitate at the bottom of the stairs, then turn and run inside the main
clubroom. Frank descended the steps, following cautiously.

By the time he reached the curtained entrance Hanford
had had ample time to conceal himself inside. Suddenly Frank
knew why the old man had not chosen to get away through the
front door, taking the truck that was parked out there. He hadn't
*wanted* to escape from Frank—somewhere inside, hidden among
the bizzare decorations of the strange oasis, Hanford was waiting
to kill him.

Frank put the gun in his belt and moved closer to the curtains.
With one hand he reached out and grabbed the fabric, pulling it
violently in the center. He let go just as the shot sounded, and
something gave the cloth a sharp tug. Instantly, then, he slipped
through at one side and knelt next to the wall, behind a table. The
gun did not sound again.

He waited, letting his eyes become accustomed to the half-
darkness. Starlike points of light gleamed from the invisible
ceiling above, casting a bluish glow across the empty tables and
chairs but not really lighting them or defining their separate
shapes. The stage area far below was caught under a single, tiny
night light from the wings. One half of the gray boulders were

illuminated by it, the rest buried in deep shadows. The pool at their base was a smooth, black patch on the white sand.

Hanford could not have imagined he'd hit him, Frank thought, or he would have made some noise or called out. Either he had not had time for a second shot as Frank had come in or had not wished to risk showing his position until Frank was close enough to make a certain target. Clenching his teeth against the fiery pain beginning to spread down his left side, Frank started cautiously between the tables, closing the distance between himself and the stage area. His eyes bored into the darkness, trying to separate the forms of trees and earthen vases from the shapeless shadows. There was a skittering noise in front of him, and he pulled the .22 up and fired. A ghostly chuckle floated to him from somewhere down front. He'd been tricked into wasting another shot. As he crawled farther forward he saw the broken saucer he had shot at, lying in the aisle. He grimaced and moved on.

When he had reached a position just a few feet from the beginning of the sand stage he stopped and carefully considered his position—the light was shining from the left side of the stage, casting the right half into thick darkness. That's where Hanford would be. Frank had an idea. Quietly, he began working in, getting as close to the open area as possible till he was finally crouching behind the last low table next to the stage. He braced his arm for a shot, fired, and cursed. He aimed and fired again—the night light went out with a crash. Immediately two heavy-bore slugs came slamming into the table, but Frank was already sprinting across the wedge of sand, throwing one of the cushionlike chairs before him and following it down behind the first large boulder.

When he opened his eyes he realized he must have passed out for an instant. The pain in his arm and left side was paralyzing now. The image of the electric light still burned on the retinas of his eyes, and he prayed that Hanford would not decide to close in on him now. At last the pain began to recede enough to let him think. He considered his chances—how many bullets expended since entering the room? Three, plus two upstairs, which meant he had one shot left. And Hanford? There had been the first shot upstairs, another in the hall, another as he left the room. That was three. The fourth through the curtains of the clubroom, and two more a moment ago. That should leave two rounds in Hanford's automatic.

Frank peered out and saw the inky water of the pool, its surface calm and still, unsuspecting of the ravenous life coursing through its depths. Quietly, he hoisted the chair in one hand.

*"Damn you!"* he cried in a voice filled with unfeigned agony. *"Oh, God!"* and he swung the thick padding up and out. It hit the pool with a flat, resounding splash, accompanied by Frank's final, despairing cry. He lay perfectly still, looking out over the edge of the rock.

Hanford took his own bait. After a moment of quiet a head appeared, dimly etched in the darkness across the pool. Frank heard the sounds of the old man's feet scrubbing against the stones and watched as the small body came erect, peering down into the water. There was a soft chuckling sound. Frank raised the revolver and aimed. He tried to tighten his finger on the trigger—and couldn't.

Sweat broke out across his face and down his body as he realized that he could not kill Hanford this way, without warning. Painfully, he straightened himself up into full view.

"I'm going to shoot, Hanford," he said and again raised the gun.

The old man, looming above him on the boulder, jerked around with a startled cry. His gun exploded and rock chips knifed into Frank's cheek and neck like thousands of tiny daggers. Holding his aim carefully, Frank squeezed the trigger of the .22. A hollow, metallic click rang sharply across the room.

With slow horror, Frank realized the final chamber had been left with no cartridge under the hammer. The gun was empty.

The knowledge of death was a cold weight in his belly as Frank looked up, waiting for the old man to kill him.

Instead, he saw Hanford struggling frantically for his own life.

Thrown off balance by Frank's unexpected appearance and his own violent reaction to it, Hanford's foothold had been loosened. He was sliding forward gradually, slipping down the face of the boulder.

Frank watched the small figure struggle, hands clutching for purchase on the hard, slick surface. At the last moment, seeing he must fall, Hanford kicked himself outward, away from the rock in an effort to leap past the pool. He fell instead into its center. When the small, shining head broke the surface it was with a sputtering cry of terror. Setting out with hard, flailing strokes, Hanford began to swim for the side. Then, suddenly, as though seized by cramps, he doubled over in the water, thrashing furiously. With a wild, half-strangled scream, he tried to swim again, but once more broke into beating, frenzied motions. His next cry, uttered half above and half under the water, made Frank's stomach lurch sickeningly.

As though entranced he came out from behind his rock and walked to the side of the pool. The body roiled on the surface, sinking, then rising again, its movements becoming weaker until at last a darker film began to spread in the water. After a while the crumpled shape sank down, still jerking and turning—but, Frank knew, not from any life that remained inside it. The hideous part was that he could not see the fish at all.

Slowly, Frank walked back up the aisle to the front of the building. As he stepped through the curtain into the lobby he fainted.

Nancy adjusted the curtains across from his bed so the light no longer fell on his face. "How is that?" she asked.

He looked around his familiar room and nodded. "Fine," he said. "Thanks, Nan." It still seemed hard to believe that he was home again, his wife in the room with him. It was the first time they'd been alone during the several hours since the police ambulance had brought him to the house. Nancy came over and sat on the edge of the bed.

"How do you feel?"

"All right," he said. "Still a little mixed up, I guess." It was the wrong time to ask, he knew, but something inside forced him ahead, promising him no peace until he found out. "Nancy," he began, "I'd like to know about—about the way—"

"About Vikki?"

He nodded. "Were you—"

"Yes, I was there. She died just after the police arrived. She knew that Hanford was finished and that you were all right—and that helped. She seemed, well—almost glad, I think."

"I see."

"She loved you very much, Frank," Nancy said very gently.

He hesitated, not knowing how to answer. "She was—"

"She was a wonderful person," the girl finished for him.

"Yes."

The late afternoon light filtered through the tilted blinds of his room, and a gentle wind stirred the curtains at the sides, bringing a fresh, sweet smell from outside that told him better than anything else he was home again. He should have been glad, he knew, at peace finally. But he was not. Lines of worry creased his face as he watched the girl beside him. So much had happened. They were almost strangers in a way—he did not know what went on inside her any more. Now he put off the moment in which he would have to ask.

"Was that Nelson on the phone a while ago?"

"Yes," Nancy told him. "He says the continuance has been granted till late next month. You're to relax and get your strength.

And he says not to worry—you're in the best legal hands in the country," she laughed.

The trial would be a bitter final dose for him, testifying, as he supposed he would have to, against Cat and Arnie Benson, the only survivors of Hanford's original gang.

"There were some more telegrams, too," she said.

What had amazed him more man anything else was the number of friends and well-wishers who had called and sent cheering messages since his return. It was not a hero's welcome, exactly, but more of an expression of faith from the people he knew. They were telling him that they were glad he'd come out okay and that they believed in him, whatever else. He felt deeply grateful and a little guilty, too, as though not sure he deserved such luck.

"Dad says if we get any more character witnesses there won't be room for the judge at the trial."

"Look, Nan," he said suddenly, then stopped, his throat strangely constricted.

"Yes?" she said, looking down at him.

"I—well, I guess you know if the trial doesn't go right I may be—gone for a while."

"Dad doesn't think so," she said, "and neither does Nelson. They both say that the armored-car people and Mrs. Fogherty will testify for you, and your record in Blaine will stand up."

"I know," he said, "but you can't tell." Again he hesitated, knowing he wasn't saying it right. "What I mean is, well—what about you?"

She leaned forward a little. "What do you mean?"

"You know—what are you going to do while all this is happening?"

For a moment she didn't answer, and then, when she did, there was understanding and a warm vibrancy in her low-pitched voice. "I'm going to stay with you, of course."

He caught her with his right arm as she came toward him, pulling her down with fierce strength. She lay beside him, resting in the curve of his arm, careful not to touch the cast on his other side. The full length of her body was warm and comforting, a gentle pressure against him. She kissed him hungrily, with sudden demand, and her kisses were hurried, yet with a sure and certain eagerness. She was his again as she had been before—but better than before, too, because he was whole at last. He was through running—through being afraid. He was sure of himself in a way he could not remember having been before.

He realized that she was crying beside him, her hands touching him gently, but when she moved her face away to look at him, it was radiant and happy.

"Would you believe it?" he whispered, "I love you as much as a man with two good arms!"

She laughed suddenly and said, "I can't believe it—you'll have to show me."

And then he showed her . . . .

THE END

*of an Original Gold Medal Novel by*
John Tomerlin

www.ingramcontent.com/pod-product-compliance
Lightning Source LLC
Chambersburg PA
CBHW052007240626
47153CB00008B/2771